BRENT PERROTTI

DESERT OF DREAMS

THE SABNARE SAGA
BOOK ONE

BRENT PERROTTI

Desert of Dreams

Book 1 of The Sabnare Saga

Desert of Dreams Hardcover ISBN: 979-8-9907713-0-7

Desert of Dreams Paperback ISBN: 979-8-9907713-1-4

Desert of Dreams Ebook ISBN: 979-8-9907713-2-1

Library of Congress Control Number: 2024927581

Cover art by Miblart (miblart.com)

https://brentperrotti.com

Spellbound Books

1st edition 2025

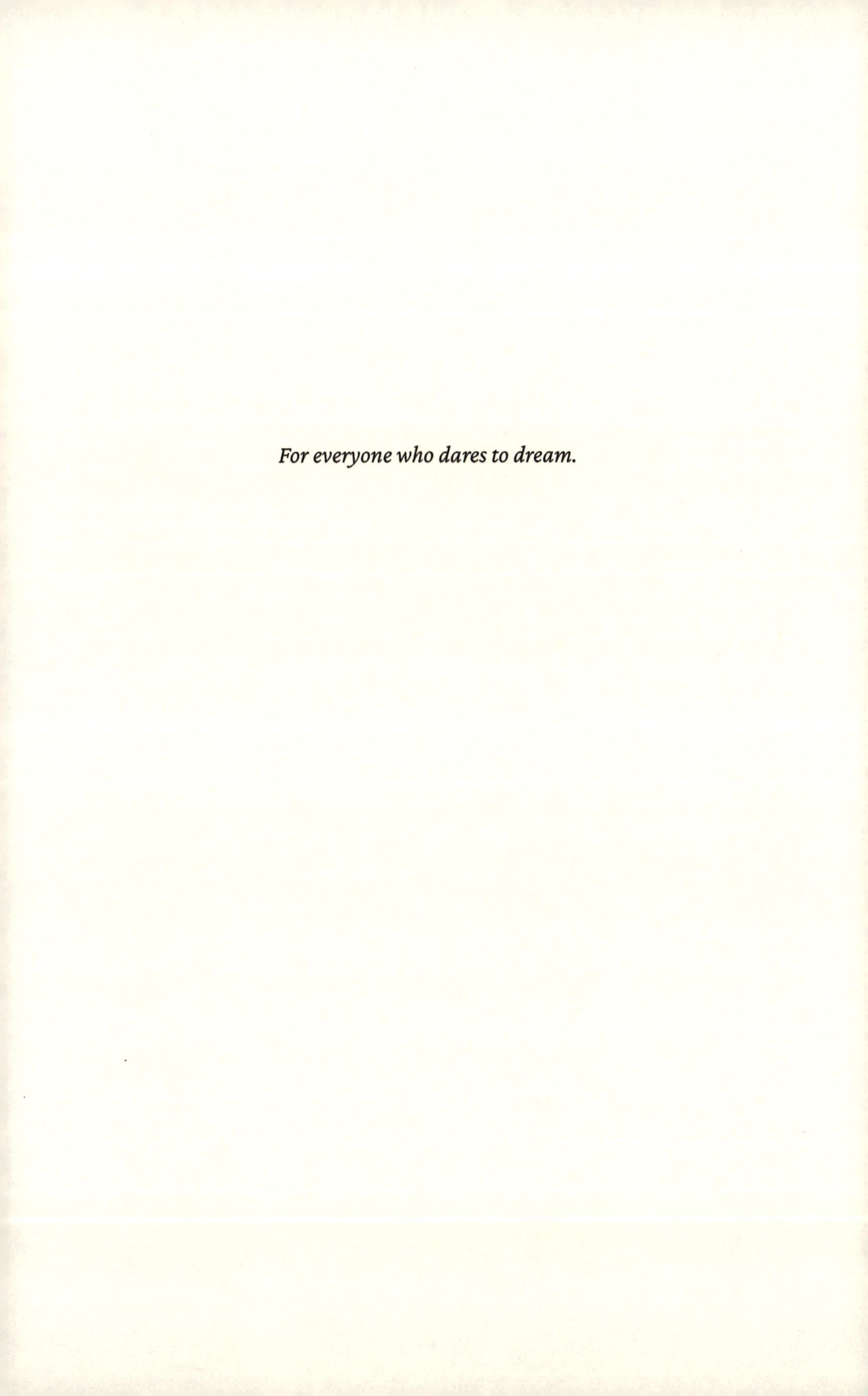

For everyone who dares to dream.

CHAPTER

ONE

The blazing hot water poured down on her, reddening her skin. Diana stood there, face to the stream. Her shower didn't wake her up as it usually did. The last few weeks, she hadn't slept well. She was used to having vivid, engaging dreams. Recently, Diana's evenings had been dreamless and empty, leaving her to wake, not feeling refreshed. It wasn't something that she had much time to think about, she had to get ready for her day.

She turned off the water, wrapped a towel around herself, and returned to her room. She entered her room, reached over to her iPod dock, and hit shuffle. Instantly, RuPaul's *If I Dream* began to play through the speakers of her dock as she stood in front of the closet, picking out clothes. She shimmied into a well-worn pair of jeans and pulled a t-shirt featuring a local drag queen off of a hanger.

She stepped past piles of clean laundry that seemed to be ever engulfing her floor and made her way over to a glass terrarium. She turned on the light sitting on the hood and opened the top of the glass.

"Good morning boys," she said as she went in and tidied up the tank, "Looks like we had an eventful evening."

She chuckled to herself; it never ceased to amaze her that two hermit crabs could achieve so much mayhem in one evening. Their food dish was turned over. Extra shells were flung about the tank. Even their climbing rope lay on the ground.

After replacing the food dish and straightening up the tank, she did a scan to find her two crabs. She spotted the smaller of her two hermit crabs, Carl, in the cave that was in the back corner of the tank. It didn't take her long to find the other crab, Sigmund, in his favorite hiding place. He was curled up in his shell in the hanging moss pit. She grabbed the misting bottle and gave a few sprays to the tank and moss pit.

As she sprayed, Diana saw a movement in the sand out of the corner of her eye. She looked closer but couldn't see what would cause such a disturbance. She shrugged it off, chalking it up to her lack of a restful night's sleep. She closed the lid so as not to let all of the humidity out of the tank. Diana watched as Carl scuttled out of the cave. He headed directly for the green apple slices that were his favorite treat and began to rip off pieces with his little claw. He chirped with delight as the bits of apple reached his mouthpieces.

"Alright boys, enjoy your food," she said, stepping back from the tank, "Try not to wreck the place too bad."

She knew that she had asked them for more than they could possibly deliver. Even so, that was part of their charm, and her crabs delighted her. Diana could watch them for hours, climbing about and digging in the sand. She always was a bit envious of them getting to play in the sand all night, as they are mostly nocturnal. Life on the beach must be nice, she thought. Living just north of Chicago didn't really afford her a beach lifestyle.

Diana began to shuffle through one of the many piles of clean laundry that littered her floor for a pair of socks. She finally got them on and reached for a pair of sneakers that she slid on without untying. She wiggled and danced until her heels were finally in, and the shoe was on comfortably. She headed for the door, nearly tripping over a basket full of unfinished knitting projects with sloppy, uneven stitches.

Diana headed down the stairs. On the final step, she used her momentum and spun around, holding the spiral part of the banister, and shot into the kitchen. Her hand reached for the remote on the counter, and with a click, the TV sprang to life. The familiar faces of the local news anchors greeted her with their usual banter. She plopped herself down in a chair at the table, where a note from her mother was waiting.

> Diana,
>
> I had to go into work. It looks like it will be a long day, I'm afraid you'll have to fend for yourself. There is plenty of food in the fridge. Good luck today! Wish I could be there.
>
> Love, Mom

Diana reread the note. Her mother, Selene, worked in a fancy hotel downtown as a maid, and it kept her very busy. For as long as Diana could remember, her mother had always been very consumed by her work. She very rarely made it to any of the things Diana participated in growing up. Everything from plays and recitals to sporting events. Diana always wished her mother would have been more present as she grew up, even if she never excelled in any of the things she tried. Even though today's reveal came as no surprise, she was still filled with disappointment. That feeling never truly passed.

She crumpled up the note and tossed it into the trash can. She hopped out of her chair and opened the freezer, removing a package of frozen waffles. She pulled out two waffles as she walked over to the toaster.

As Diana waited for the toaster to do its work, she went about the humble kitchen, gathering all she needed for her meal. Diana had always liked the charming kitchen with its yellow-painted walls.

She was especially fond of the wallpaper border that ran along the ceiling featuring happy cows in a field. Selene was very fond of cows. In fact, the kitchen was full of them. Cows were featured on the drapes and dishtowels, but Diana had a special fondness for the cow oven mitts that looked like little puppets.

As Diana finished grabbing the last few items, she listened to the news anchors mention a fistfight had broken out the night before at a local grocery store. It seemed that these strange random acts of violence were becoming all too frequent within the last few weeks. None of which you would expect, each location becoming stranger with each day. Everywhere from church functions and ice cream shops to Build-A-Bear workshops. None of them seemed to follow any kind of set patterns other than people getting easily agitated with little to no provocation. Every day, the reported number of incidents grew in frequency and intensity.

The sound of the toaster snapped her out of her thoughts. After fetching the waffles, she sat back down and proceeded to pour strawberry syrup all over, filling each individual square before moving back over the middle and letting the syrup cascade down the sides of the waffles and pooling on the plate. Diana took a bite and savored the sweetness of the strawberry, enjoying her breakfast and watching the news.

Stories about a new birth at the Lincoln Park Zoo, free days at the museums, and an upcoming visit from the President were all relayed. There was even a mention of the charity volleyball tournament that Diana was going to be participating in that day and that the station would be there covering the event.

Diana began to clear up her mess while thinking about the coverage of the tournament. There was a flick of hope that perhaps, in a small way, her mom might get to see a bit of her participating in the tournament. She set the DVR for the rest of the day's news to be sure she didn't miss any potential footage of her. She glanced at the clock on the stove. "I better finish getting ready," she said aloud to no one, and with that, headed back up to her room to grab her volleyball bag.

Diana stepped outside and locked the door. The warmth of the sun caressed her tan skin as she stepped down off the stoop. The scent of flowers tickled her nose. Her mother's garden was in full bloom. Flower beds bordered the front of the house while overflowing baskets hung from the window awnings. For as busy as her mom was, Diana could never figure out how she had the time to tend to such an impressive garden.

She wasn't able to dwell on the manner long, for a buzzing sound snapped her back to reality. A chill ran down her, and she froze in place. Her eyes searched for the origin of the buzzing, and then she saw it was bees.

Bees had terrified her since she was a little girl, and had accidentally disturbed a hive. They swarmed and stung her multiple times. Luckily, she wasn't allergic, but it did send her to the hospital. Several bees were flying about from flower to flower. Even though many years had passed, Diana couldn't shake her fear. Intellectually, she knew that it was a rare occurrence and that she didn't really have anything to fear from bees visiting their garden.

As she regained some composure, she continued down the path toward the sidewalk. Just as she was almost to the sidewalk, she heard more buzzing and felt something delicately touch her hand. Again, she froze and slowly moved her hand to better see what happened. There, perched on her left hand, was a honey bee. The color drained from her face, and she let out a blood-curdling scream and took off down the sidewalk.

Diana slowed down to catch her breath several blocks away. Diana rounded the corner and could now see her destination. She walked up the pathway towards the front door of the large single-family home of her friend Molly. Molly had been her best friend since they were young, like sisters. Diana had practically grown up at Molly's home, with her mother constantly working, Molly's family would look after her.

She reached out and rang the doorbell. A moment later, the door opened, revealing Molly's father. He was a tall man in his late 40s with a slight dusting of gray in his rusty hair. He was wearing an emerald green cabled sweater vest. He was known for his sweater vests; they were his favorite part of his wardrobe.

"Hello Mr. Madigan, is Molly ready yet?" She greeted him.

"Diana, my other daughter, how good to see you!" He said, pulling her in for a hug, "It's been far too long."

They stepped inside, and he closed the door behind them.

"Molly is in her room," he said, motioning towards the stairs.

"Thanks Mr. Madigan," Diana said as she moved towards the stairs.

Diana made her way up the stairs and down the hallway. The Madigans had adorable family photos hanging down the hallway. There was a picture of Molly from around third grade. Another of Molly's older brother and some of her grandparents. At the end of the hallway next to Molly's room was Diana's favorite picture. It was a complete family photo featuring Molly and her brother and parents. Both sets of grandparents were present in the photo, along with aunts, uncles, and cousins. Next to a young Molly was a young Diana.

Diana smiled, remembering this day, it was a Madigan family reunion. Once again, Diana's mother was working, so she was tagging along. She remembered feeling out of place and a sense of intruding where she didn't belong. Not that any of the Madigans felt that way it was just her own insecurities intruding on her thought space. When it was time for the family photo to be taken, Diana remembered hanging back and watching everyone get arranged. Molly's mother was taking it all in from her spot in the photo. Looking the group up and down when she looked over to Diana standing off to the side.

"Diana," she called out, "Come stand next to Molly." Diana hesitated and looked down at the ground.

"Just a moment," Mrs. Madigan said to the group as she broke from the formation and headed over to where Diana was standing. Once she reached where Diana was, she kneeled in front of her and cupped her hand within her own.

"Diana, sweetie, why don't you want to come be a part of the picture," she asked softly. Diana looked up at her. Her face was filled with love and concern.

"It's supposed to be for family," she replied, "and I'm not family."

"Sweetheart, I want to tell you something about family," she said, squeezing Diana's hands. "Family comes in many forms; there is the family you have by blood, and there is the family you receive when two people marry." She paused, looking at Diana, who was staring down at the ground again. She gently placed her hand under her chin and guided her head up until they were looking eye to eye. "Then there is the family you choose," she continued, "There may not be blood or papers that say you are related, but what is there is love. That's the bond that truly makes a family," she paused to smile at Diana, "so please help me get a picture that shows my whole family."

"Okay," Diana said, wiping away tears, "I'll be in the picture."

"Good, let's join the others." Mrs. Madigan walked Diana over, holding her hand, and placed her next to Molly and in front of Mr. Madigan. Mr. Madigan placed his hand on her shoulder as the picture was taken.

Diana smiled as she finished looking over the photo and turned her attention to the door to Molly's room. She knocked on the door with the secret knock they had developed many years ago.

"Come in," came a call from inside. Diana turned the knob and let herself in. She stepped into the room. Molly's room was larger than Diana's and much more organized than she'd ever seen her own. She scanned the room and found Molly sitting at her vanity, finishing her makeup. Diana walked over to her side.

"You do know we are about to get all sweaty playing volleyball, right?" Diana teased her friend.

Molly turned to smirk at her friend. Tossing her fiery red hair over her shoulder.

"Well, I wouldn't want people to think the charity we are playing for is me," she joked.

Diana laughed. She also knew that it wouldn't be Molly without her signature green eye shadow. Diana was always amazed at how effortless Molly made it all look with her beautiful fair skin and bright, full, wavy hair that was never out of place. Diana thought about her ongoing battle of the frizz. It wasn't as bad as she made it out to be, but it was always just frizzed enough not to achieve the look she was going for. That's why, most days, hers ended up in a simple ponytail.

Molly put the final touches on her makeup and stepped away from her vanity. She walked over and hugged Diana.

"You ready for this?" Molly asked.

"You bet, athletic superstar Diana, ready to enter the fray," she joked, barely containing her laughter.

Diana enjoyed sports, but like most things, she sure didn't excel at them. She turned to look at Molly's collection of trophies, filling an entire bookcase next to her vanity. Molly had won trophies for golf, softball, track, and basically every other sport she'd ever played. Also hanging from the shelves were a multitude of ribbons that were as varied as her trophies. Molly had won a ribbon in every science fair she had ever entered, unlike Diana, who somehow almost burnt down the gym with a paper mâché volcano in the third grade. She wasn't forced to participate in the mandatory science fairs after that.

Molly finished grabbing all the things she needed and loaded them in her duffle bag. She gave the room a final scan and shuffled through her bag one more time while muttering to herself, listing everything she needed.

"Well, I guess I have all I need," Molly said, turning to Diana, "Shall we head out?"

"Definitely," Diana replied, "We don't want to get stuck using the reject changing tents."

"Oh yeah, last year was horrendous."

Molly shuddered, remembering the tents near the port-a-potty that started leaking. "On the bright side, I did get to buy this cute new bag," she quipped.

The girls laughed as they headed for the door. They headed down the stairs and towards the front door. As they reached the door, Molly turned and called out to her parents.

"Mom, Dad, we're leaving."

"Okay girls, be safe," Mrs. Madigan said as she peered out from the living room, "we will see you in a little while."

"Bye Mrs. Madigan," Diana said as she headed out the door with Molly following behind her. They headed over to Molly's gold convertible. They tossed their bags in the back seat and got settled. Molly backed out of the driveway and headed to the beach.

Lake Michigan may not be tropical, but Diana was still looking forward to it. The wind danced with their hair as the car made its way towards the beach.

Molly turned down a street lined with million-dollar homes. This was not the part of Evanston that Diana was used to, but the houses were beautiful. They came to a stop sign as an elderly woman crossed the street with her cane. A man coming from the opposite direction came to a stop in his sports car. The older woman continued to cross in front of the sports car as Molly proceeded forward. The man began blaring his horn at the woman as she crossed. The woman turned and began to hit the hood of the man's car with her cane. He opened his door to get out and yell at the woman. With one quick motion, the woman smashed off his side mirror and began to hit him in the leg. Diana turned in her seat to watch as the man jumped back in his car and drove off.

"Did you see that?" Diana asked.

"That was crazy," Molly said, "What's been happening lately?"

The girls tried to put the scene out of their minds and continued on their way. Molly made the final turn towards the venue. As they pulled into the parking lot, it was already starting to fill up. They could easily spot the news vans that were parked there to cover the event, along with the vans belonging to the charity right up front. There was even a section reserved for several food trucks that would be catering the event. As they made their way down the lane, a car began to pull out of a spot near the entrance to the beach. Molly waited for the car to finish, then promptly claimed the spot.

Molly gathered their bags from the back as Diana made her way toward the entrance. She looked around for the location of the registration tent. Diana spotted a frazzled-looking man with a clipboard and an earpiece.

"Excuse me, sir," Diana said, walking up to the man, "can you tell us where the registration tent is?" The man looked her over. Finally, looking down the end of his nose through his glasses, he replied.

"Which registration are you looking for? Are you volunteers?"

"No, we are signed up to play in the tournament," Diana replied.

"They must have really needed bodies this year," he said, barely glancing at her, "continue down this row till it ends and take a right. "Registration for," he paused and glanced at her once more, "athletes will be at the end." Without another word, he took off talking into his earpiece.

Diana stood there in disbelief, and the man had walked away before she could say anything to him about his unacceptable behavior. A part of her understood the anger of that old lady with the cane. Diana brushed off his comments and put it out of her mind as Molly walked over to her.

"Were you able to figure out where we need to be?"

"Yeah," Diana said, trying to shake off the feeling the clipboard man left her with, "it's this way."

Diana guided Molly as they made their way through the crowds towards the tent so they could sign in. They walked up to the line coming from the tent and saw a woman in glasses with dull, frizzy brown hair. She was wearing a t-shirt prominently featuring cats. Her most defining feature was her full, rosy cheeks and warm, radiant smile that almost felt like a hug. The girls finally stepped up to the table, and the woman greeted them with her infectious smile.

"Hello girls, can I have your names, please?"

"Molly Madigan"

"Diana Mendoza"

The woman scanned and shuffled through her papers, looking for the names. After a bit of searching, she perked up.

"Well, here we are, ladies," she said, handing them t-shirts and numbers, "looks like you are both on the purple team." The woman paused as she looked Diana directly in the eyes and let out another of her infectious smiles. "Looks like the shirt will match your beautiful eyes."

"Uh, yeah, thanks," Diana stammered as she took her shirt and number, trying to avoid direct eye contact. This was nothing new for her, as ordinary as she was in almost every way, there was one thing about her that did stand out. Her eyes. She had bright, crystal-clear purple eyes that always brought her attention. When she was little, kids would tease her for being different, and girls were mean to her due to their jealousy. Eventually, she grew to love her eye color, but every once in a while, when mentioned by people, it made her a bit embarrassed.

"Looks like you girls will be starting on court three, most of your team should be there already," said the woman, "Good luck, and have fun."

They stepped back from the table and rejoined the herds of people making their way towards the courts and changing tents. Molly spotted the changing tents, and lucky for them, there didn't appear to be a line. The girls stepped into the tents and changed into their athletic gear, complete with their new team shirts.

Diana exited the tent to find Molly already finished and waiting for her. Of course, Molly looked pin-up perfect, like she fell off a Wheaties box. Her near effortless perfection would be annoying if she wasn't also the kindest person in the world and completely oblivious to how others saw her. Diana felt tremendously frumpy next to her friend. However, Molly's smile was enough to forget about being self-conscious. The pair headed towards their court to get ready for their match.

They approached the court and spotted four other people in purple shirts standing in front of what appeared to be a referee. Diana scanned the faces of the purple team. There were two guys that she didn't know. One had shaggy blond hair, while the other was taller with chestnut hair in a spiky undercut. They both had trim athletic builds and appeared to be a couple since they were holding hands as they listened to the referee. The other two members of the team were girls that she recognized from high school but didn't know very well. The first was Drea Chang, the shortest member of the team she stood no higher than 5'2'' with short hair with the right side of her head shaved. From what Diana could recall, Drea had been active with several sports teams and excelled in most of them. The other girl was wearing her hair in two afro puffs. Diana immediately recognized her as Olivia Hemsley. Olivia was the valedictorian of their graduating class and had received a full scholarship to Howard University in Washington, DC.

Diana and Molly joined the group and checked in. Molly chatted with Drea and Olivia, who she had honors classes with back in high school. Diana went to introduce herself to the boys.

"Hi, I'm Diana," she said, reaching out her hand.

The shaggy-haired guy shook her hand.

"Nice to meet you I'm Henry, and this is my boyfriend, Grant."

Grant shook Diana's hand.

"What made you join the tournament today?" Diana asked.

"We just moved here from New York and thought it would be a fun way to meet people," Grant said. "How about you?"

"Molly and I do it every year. It's a great cause, and I love any excuse to be at the beach, even if I'm not nearly as skilled at volleyball as she is."

Diana was excited at the group dynamic; they all got on really well. Best of all, they had a nice mix of skill levels.

The sound of the loudspeakers brought everyone's attention to the grandstand of the volleyball courts. Diana recognized the woman on stage from before at the registration tent. The woman began to address the crowd with the microphone.

"Hello everyone, and welcome to Strong Families Strong Futures annual charity fundraiser volleyball tournament. My name is Nancy Christiansen, and I'm the president and founder of Strong Families Strong Futures. Our organization is focused on providing numerous services that strengthen the family unit. We work within communities to help provide daycare, family counseling, adoption assistance, and much more. We believe that the family is the key to success, and that's why we reach out to help all types of families, whether they be traditional, single-parent, or same-sex couples, to reach their full potential. I'd like to thank you all again for your generous support let's have fun today and have some incredible matches!"

Nancy gave one of her smiles while exiting the stage as the crowd cheered.

The scent of the water reached Diana's nose as the wind came in from the lake. Stepping onto the court, digging her toes in the sand, feeling truly at home. She smiled with one side of her mouth and thought of Carl and Sigmund. They're not the only ones playing in the sand today. She chuckled to herself as she prepared for the tournament to start.

TWO

The day's tournament had been going strong. Game after game, point after point. The adrenaline surged through Diana's veins. She turned to Molly and saw her grinning, eyes lit up with focus and drive. After a few close calls, their team had really solidified as a unit and had fought all the way to the final match. The sun hung lower in the sky, preparing to set. Diana's team was sweaty and bruised. Everyone on the purple team was feeling the strain, but they managed to somehow keep the positivity alive.

They were gathered on the bench awaiting the final team's arrival, enjoying a much-needed and well-deserved water break. As they were casually chatting, Molly pointed towards the other side of the court. Everyone directed their attention at the incoming team clad in orange.

They made their way to the net to greet their latest opponents. However, the orange team wasn't sharing in the camaraderie and sportsmanship. A tall blonde girl dressed in orange looked down her nose at Diana's outstretched hand as if touching it would be the equivalent of bathing in a sewer. This was the kindest of the interactions with the orange team. Each of them was more off-putting than the last. Diana found the reaction quite strange for participants in a charity event. It was as if they were irritated just by being there and being involved, much less having to interact with other people.

The teams got into position for the start of the game. The orange team was serving first. Diana stood front and center by the net, with Molly on her left and Grant to her right. The referee blew the whistle, and the final match was underway. The opposing team served the ball. The game was fast-paced. Each team not wanting to give up a point. The ball drifted to the back row of the purple team, and Olivia positioned herself under it and bumped it back to the front row, and Molly set it back over the net. A curly-haired girl in the front leapt up and spiked it back over, slamming it directly into Diana's face. The force momentarily blinded her as the ball rebounded from her face into the net and onto the ground.

"That's one way to get your head in the game," sneered the curly-haired girl as she turned away from the net. Molly ran over to Diana to check on her.

"Oh my god, are you okay," the concern in her voice was palpable.

Diana's vision was a blur of colors she'd never seen before as she regained her vision and composure.

"Yeah, I'm fine," she said, smiling at her friend as she shook herself out and rubbed her nose, "let's do this!" The intensity of the match never let up. Each team continued to score points, never letting the other pull too far ahead.

It was the purple team's turn to serve. Luckily, it was Drea's turn to serve, as she was the best at the position on the team. As she waited for Drea, Diana felt how tired her body was. She took a long, deep breath in. She felt the coolness of the lake-side air filling her lungs as dusk was winning its battle with the day. A calm came over her entire body, and her mind became clear. She felt the sand between her toes, and it was as if she could sense each individual grain and its movements. She was connected as if the entire beach was an extension of herself, feeling the pulse of all the players around her. Diana assumed it was the adrenaline of the game coursing through her, bringing her focus back to the match at hand.

Drea served the ball, and it flew over the net. The ball was returned by the orange team. Diana watched as the ball soared over the net and headed right in her direction. She focused on the ball and prepared to set it. Hands in the air, she reached for the ball. She extended herself. All of her focus was on reaching the ball. All she wanted was to reach the ball. Before she could jump, a strange, warm sensation flowed throughout her body. It felt as if the sand itself was lifting her towards the ball. She glanced down at her feet, and indeed, the sand had actually lifted her a foot off the ground. Startled, Diana lost her focus, and the sand collapsed under her. Unfortunately, her momentum kept her going, and her legs slipped out from under her, and she ended up butt planted firmly in the sand as the volleyball landed beside her.

The referee's whistle blared.

"Game point, the orange team is the winner."

The crowd erupted into cheers. Diana could barely hear them, as if she was caught in a vacuum of her own thoughts. She was relentlessly replaying the scene over and over in her mind, trying to figure out what happened. Was it all in her head? A trick of the light? It felt real. Was it even possible? She continued to sit there in the sand, lost in thought, with questions zooming around her brain. She barely noticed that the rest of her team had converged around her. Molly reached out her hand to Diana, bringing her back from inside her head. She took Molly's hand as she hoisted her to her feet. She looked into all their smiling faces.

"Don't be so hard on yourself," Molly said, "It's not a big deal."

"I know it's just that..."

"No, really girl," Grant interrupted, "We all had fun, win or lose."

"Yeah, it's not about that, it's..."

"Well then, we should all go out and celebrate, "Olivia chimed in.

Diana let out a sigh. She realized that she was never going to be able to explain what was happening with everyone in celebration mode. It was apparent that no one saw what happened, or if they did, it wasn't something that stood out as anything out of the ordinary. She tried to bring herself to be fully present in the moment that the rest of her team was sharing. She threw on a fake smile and tried to hide the hurricane of concern spiraling in her head. Everyone stopped focusing on trying to cheer her up; it appeared to be working. Until she turned to face Molly. Molly's usually jubilant face had lost its normal glow, and her brow was furrowed in concern. Crap, she thought. She was hoping Molly would have bought her act, but she should have known better. Molly knew her too well. The fact that Diana was trying so hard to make her think everything was okay was the biggest sign that it was anything but.

As the rest of the team excitedly made plans to go out and celebrate, Molly told them that she and Diana had other plans. They all exchanged contact information and promised a rain check. Diana and Molly waved as their teammates headed towards the parking lot and out of sight.

Diana led Molly towards the rocks by the water. It was one of her favorite spots along the beach. The sky was turning shades of pink and purple like a watercolor made with masterful brushstrokes. Reflections of the rising moon danced across the waves till it touched the water's edge. The only sound, the gentle swooshing of the water running over the sand and the sounds of the tournament winding down, was a low rumble in the distance. The girls settled on the rocks and sat in each other's silence. Molly knew that Diana would be the one to start the conversation. After a few minutes, Diana finally broke the silence.

"Did anything ever happen to you that you couldn't explain?" Diana asked, moving hair out of her face.

"Like what," asked Molly. Diana gazed at the moon as it journeyed higher into the darkening sky.

"I'm not sure how to explain it," she started, "or if it even really happened." Diana tried to organize her thoughts. "It was as if the sand lifted me up to meet the ball, and then it just disappeared."

Molly's face scrunched with a mix of worry and compassion for her friend as she listened.

"My whole life, I've never excelled at anything," Diana continued, "I've tried my hand at everything, but nothing has ever been fulfilling. Then this thing happens that I can barely even put into words how it felt and what it could mean. And if this thing did happen, I can only wonder why it would happen to me." Diana hung her head.

"Well, I'm not sure what happened," Molly started, "but there is one thing I know for sure." She looked at Diana, who was reluctant to meet her gaze. "You're completely wrong about not excelling at anything. One of the greatest things about you is your friendship. You are kind and supportive; you've never not been there for me." Molly placed her hand on Diana's leg before continuing. "So, whatever happened, I'd have to believe it happened for a reason. Just because you feel you haven't found your calling yet doesn't mean it's true. Perhaps it's indicative that there has been a larger plan for you all along, something beyond your wildest dreams." Diana looked at her friend and placed her hand on top of hers.

"Do you really think there is a plan for me?"

Molly gave a radiant, heartfelt smile. "Diana, I can honestly say there is more to you than you know, and once you fully embrace your true self, everything will change."

Diana was starting to feel better. Molly always had a way of words and a way of looking at the world that Diana envied. With as much as she was unsure of, there was one thing she knew deep within her, like a primal memory. She knew that having Molly as a friend was the greatest bit of luck she ever had and to never take that for granted.

The friends sat there a little longer, gazing at the moon as it sat higher above them. Each confidant that they were the luckier of the pair for having the other. These were the moments that mattered, together with nothing but the water crashing against the rocks and an owl hooting in the distance.

Molly offered to drive Diana home. Diana thanked her but told her that she wanted to walk home. The girls hugged, and Molly took off. Diana lingered on the beach a while longer. She walked along the shore, dragging her toes in the sand behind her as she walked. As she continued along, she'd stop and stand on her tiptoes, trying to raise herself up like before. After several attempts, she decided that it was time to head home.

She made her way through the familiar streets she'd known her whole life. Everything felt familiar and normal, but for some reason, she was having a hard time believing that everything was as it had always been. Just like this street, there was the fabric store that had been there for decades, but just a few storefronts up, there was a new and trendy wine shop that had recently opened. Things change, and life shakes you up. Diana couldn't help but feel like her life had been rather stagnant. Perhaps this was a way to revitalize her, but what was it? Even now, she wasn't sure that it wasn't all just an illusion. She never had run across a story about a person that sand lifted into the air. It had to be something more rational. She must have jumped and not realized it, and the sand she saw was kicked up, and the perspective played a trick on her, just like in the crab tank earlier. Every step closer to home made her more confident that it had all been a mistake. Nothing like the crisp night air to bring back a bit of clarity.

As she turned a corner, she passed a rather large window reflecting the light of the moon towards her. Stopping to look at the window, she saw herself illuminated in the moon's soft embrace. There was something powerful seeing herself bathed in the moonlight, like an aura of armor surrounding and empowering her. She let the image totally encompass her and felt all of her worry and confusion dissipate into the shadows of night. For the first time since the incident, she felt grounded and centered from the moon's energy. She finally felt like herself again. Now, she could focus on the truly pressing problem that would face her when she got home. What kind of pizza would she order for dinner?

THREE

"Mom, I'm home," Diana called, dropping her keys on the table by the door, "Mom, are you home?" Diana waited for a reply. Silence came from the house. Selene still wasn't home, which wasn't unusual. Diana had the house to herself. She entered the kitchen, walked over to the pantry, and pulled out the folder of take-out menus from the shelf. She flipped through the menus as if she didn't know exactly which pizza place she was going to order from. She pulled out the menu of her favorite pizzeria. Diana dialed the number and ordered her regular order of pepperoni and bacon on a triple-thin crust.

With the pizza ordered, she headed upstairs to change into something more appropriate for lounging around the house. Donning yoga pants, an oversized sweatshirt, and some hand-knit wool socks, she was now ready for her evening. While she waited, she walked over to the crab tank to turn off the light for the evening, and then she decided to put away some of the clean laundry that had been living on her floor for so long it should have been paying rent.

The doorbell rang, and she went and retrieved her pizza and then returned to her room. Diana settled into her bed with her pizza and pop and turned on Netflix so she could catch up on her shows. The pizza was fresh, cheese bubbling as she opened the lid. The familiar scent of bacon greeted her nose as she closed her eyes and took it in. The pepperoni had just the right amount of kick to it as she took a bite. She crunched through the crispy crust. *This,* she thought, *is how you spend an evening.* She pressed play and settled in for her evening of bingeing.

A few hours into her pizza and movie night, she had finished the most current season of her favorite show. She began to scroll through the menu screen, looking for what to watch next. As she was trying to decide between a romantic comedy or science fiction thriller, she thought she heard a noise, like someone walking around coming from downstairs. She stopped scrolling and listened. She thought she heard something again. It must be Mom coming home, she thought to herself.

"Mom?" she called out, walking over to her door. "Mom, are you home?" She paused and listened for a reply. None came. *Oh well, I must have imagined it.* But then she heard it again. Diana knew that she hadn't made it up this time. The sound of footsteps and rustling. There was definitely something downstairs. She slowly and quietly made her way down the hall to the top of the stairs. She waited. She didn't hear anything. She started to make her way down the stairs, going slowly to not make them creak.

She made her way around the ground floor. Her breath began to quicken. The sound of the air escaping her nose seemed all too loud. Her heartbeat intensified as she walked through the kitchen towards the basement door. She leaned in, placing her ear against the door. She could barely hear anything over the beating of her own heart.

She opened the door as slowly as possible. She took the stairs slowly as she descended into the unknown darkness. At the bottom of the stairs, she turned on the light. She reached for a shovel that was leaning against the wall and made her way into the basement. The semi-finished basement had a small area for entertaining right when you stepped in. Diana walked past the couch towards the back half of the basement that was utilized for storage. She opened the door that divided the sections of the basement. She passed boxes of Christmas decorations and ones containing old childhood toys. She looked more closely at a box of crafting supplies. It appeared that a few boxes had toppled over. A wave of relief rushed over her. She knew those boxes had been stacked poorly. She leaned the shovel against the shelves, picked up the boxes that had fallen, and stacked them back up in a more stable manner.

Just as she finished cleaning up the mess of boxes, she turned to head back upstairs when she heard a noise at the far end of the basement. She picked up the shovel. She had one hand on the grip and the other on the shaft close to the blade. She moved towards the noise. Her muscles tensed, and her hands began to tremble.

She came around the corner of the wall and couldn't believe her eyes. There was a creature standing there on all fours. It had a trunk-like nose and a long tail flicking behind it. Its stance looked like it was ready to pounce. Diana let out a scream as she raised the shovel over her head, ready to strike. She began to swing the shovel down when something stopped its momentum. She turned her head to see a young, white-haired man with one fist clenched on the shovel.

"I wouldn't do that," he said, reaching into a pouch on his hip. Before Diana had time to react, he threw some kind of gritty purple powder into her face. Her eyes became heavy, and her mind began to quiet. She lost grip of the shovel as exhaustion set in, and she fell to her knees before her body fully collapsed on the floor. The man and creature hovering over her was the last thing she saw before blacking out completely.

FOUR

Diana was sitting in a large, leather wingback chair next to a roaring fireplace. The wood crackled, releasing a soothing, smokey lavender scent into the air as it burned. She looked around. There were several other chairs all situated around the fire. The walls were tall and made of what appeared to be some kind of purple stone. The stones seemed to flicker and glow. The room was massive. She felt almost insignificant and dwarfed by the size of it all. Her best guess was that it was some sort of palace. Her eyes met a beautiful tapestry of a dragon, with immaculate stitching, that hung proudly over the mantle.

The fire suddenly raged, embers bursting into the air. The flames grew larger, dancing with an increasing wildness. The flames began to swirl out of the fireplace, like a long tentacle, towards the chair opposite her. The flames leapt from the logs, leaving the fireplace completely, and continued to spin in the chair. The fire gave one last great flare before expanding out into nothing, revealing a shadowy figure of a man, lit only by the embers left in the fireplace by the exiting fire. Diana couldn't make out any distinct features. Just a flash of white hair and a beard in the soft glow. There was still something familiar about the man sitting across from her. Something comforting.

"Diana," the man spoke, "it is good to see you." His voice was kind. Diana let herself relax slightly, as confused as she was, as she looked across the room.

"Who are you," she asked, "do I know you?"

"The important thing is that I know you, and I'm here to prepare you."

"Prepare me? Prepare me for what?"

"There is more to you than you've ever dreamed. Your whole world is about to change, and I'm afraid that is all my fault."

Diana's face twisted in confusion, but confusion was overtaken by intrigue. She continued listening carefully to what he had to say, not wanting to miss a word.

"Things have been in motion long before you were born. A great danger lies ahead. I always dreamed that it wouldn't come to this. I did everything in my power to protect you so that you might never have to shoulder this burden. Know that your purpose in life is about to become clear, and you are capable of facing the trials ahead, but you will need to believe in yourself fully." He paused. "I'm sorry. What is about to be asked of you isn't fair, but there is no one else who can take on this role."

"What do you mean danger?" Diana stammered. "What's been in motion? What role?"

The floor began to shake. Diana grasped the arms of the chair, and the man spoke again.

"We are out of time," he said as his feet began to disappear like embers in the wind. "Be brave, trust in yourself, and accept help when you need it." Diana watched as he continued to disappear back into the fireplace.

"Who are you," she called out, "will I see you again?"

"That, my dear, is dependent on you." He continued to dissolve back into embers, drifting into the fireplace until he was gone. The room began to shake more violently than before until the room burst apart. The pieces of the room began floating in a void. She plummeted past floating chairs and chunks of stone wall. Her piercing scream shifted into a blood-curdling wail, like that of a banshee, as her falling began to pick up momentum. The darkness of the void was broken by a pinpoint of light. She plummeted towards the light as it overtook the darkness, and her speed became reckless. The light broke, and she passed through it like a ring and was back in endless darkness.

~

Diana opened her eyes, blinking to bring her vision into focus. She was lying in her bed, staring at the ceiling. She shuffled towards the headboard as she sat up.

"Hello honey," her mom's voice greeted her ear.

She turned to look at her mom. "Mom, you wouldn't believe what's been happening, I dreamt…" she broke off when she saw the man and creature from the basement standing behind her mother. Her mother gave a reassuring smile and placed her hand on her daughter's leg.

"I bet I would," Selene replied.

Diana was in shock, looking over the scene before her. There was a man with striking white hair that was contrasted by his tan skin. He appeared to be around twenty-five and of Middle Eastern descent. He was dressed in harem pants and robes that exposed his lean-toned upper body. She noted his strong jawline and moved up to his eyes, which had to be the biggest shock of all. His eyes were the same purple and clarity as her own. She had never run across anyone else with her color of eyes before.

Her eyes then drifted over to the creature she had seen in her basement. It appeared to be some sort of tapir. It was larger than any tapir she had ever seen. Most tapirs she had seen were black and white, but that was not the case here. This creature was a dark violet with a pink midsection. Its trunk-like snout appeared to be longer than a regular tapir's as well. Its tail flicked back and forth with a tuft of pink fur on the end like a lion's.

Perhaps the wildest thing she saw was her mother sitting there, just like everything was normal. She sat there, unfazed that some strange half-naked man in desert garb and a purple monster were standing behind her in her daughter's room. Selene sat there in a white blouse and black dress pants. She always looked classy without being flashy. Her hair pulled back in a slick ponytail. Selene was not someone who would pull your eye, but more could blend into almost any scene. It didn't matter where she went she always looked as if she belonged.

The whole day's events bombarded her. Each memory flashed past until she got out the only words that could sum up what she was feeling.

"What the fuck is going on?" She demanded. Her confusion was giving way to something deeper. Anger. It began to boil up inside of herself. Something was going on that her mom apparently knew about, but Diana had been kept in the dark.

"I'm sure this is all very confusing and that you have many questions," Selene said. "Let me start out by saying that you're special in ways most people could never imagine. That's why they are here."

Diana looked again at the man and creature in her room. The creature appeared to be smiling, happily waiting as its tail flopped up and down. At the same time, the man was much more stoic. He did not give off anything that she could read. Diana looked back at her mother.

"And who are they . . . what are they?" She asked, gesturing towards the creature.

"Well dear, this is Yume, she's a baku," she motioned to the creature. "And this is Zane. He's a sandman." Diana's face fell blank in disbelief. The words that were nonchalantly coming out of her mother's mouth, how could any of these be real?

"This doesn't make any sense," she said, running her hands through her hair.

"There's more," her mother continued, "It's about your father."

Diana's mouth parted while her head tilted, "What about my father?"

"He is also a sandman."

"Wait, what?" Diana sputtered, "That's crazy, so you're trying to tell me that my father, a man I've never met, is a sandman. Like, the guys that are supposed to put you to sleep at night?"

"Yes," Selene replied.

"That doesn't make any sense, and even if it did, if he's a sandman..." She trailed off. "That would mean that I'm a..."

"That you are a sandman," Selene replied, "Well, half sandman."

"So, I'm half sandman and half-human," Diana said, dumbfounded.

"Well," her mother grimaced, "that's not completely true."

"What do you mean that's not completely true? What am I witch, too?" Diana snarked.

"Actually, you are," her mother replied.

"That's not funny," she said. Panic in her voice. "I was only kidding!"

"Well, I'm not," Selene said. "I'm sorry that I wasn't able to tell you before," her voice quivered, "but that doesn't change the fact that everything I've told you is the truth."

Diana was reeling from the bombs that had been dropped on her. Her body felt weak. She didn't think that she could even stand if she tried. How could she be expected to believe anything that she just heard? Granted, the baku sitting in her room incessantly smiling at her did seem pretty indisputable.

"This isn't real, nothing about me has ever been special," Diana said once she regained her thoughts. "Also, I think I would've known if you were a witch, Mom."

"Keeping this hidden from you has been the hardest thing I've ever had to do." Diana could see tears forming in her mother's eyes.

"There are things I never got to do with you. Get you your first robes and teach you your first spell. I had to isolate us from the rest of my family." Tears freely flowed down Selene's face. "My biggest regret of all is in trying to protect you; I isolated myself from you as well."

Diana had never seen her mother like this. Her mother was always picture-perfect. Always composed, always strong. She had the ability to make their life appear like a Hallmark ad to anyone looking. Maybe she was a witch after all. She got herself up, walked over to her mom, and placed her hand on her shoulder.

"It's going to be okay we will get this all sorted out," she said, only half believing the words as they left her mouth.

Selene pulled her daughter in for a hug, beginning to sob. Diana couldn't remember the last time they hugged each other like this. The longer they held it, the harder it was for Diana to hold back her emotions. She was confused and angry, but tears started to stream down her face as well. These were the moments she had needed so desperately to share with her mom. In this moment, she didn't feel alone and neglected as she had become accustomed. It wasn't going to fix everything, but it was a start, and she was grateful for this moment.

The mother-daughter pair released themselves from the hug and got themselves settled. Diana saw that Zane and Yume were standing patiently. Then, something dawned on her as she looked at them. She turned to address them.

"Okay," Diana sighed. "So, I'm a sandman and a witch." The craziness of those words stuck in her mind. "Why are you here?" She asked. "There must be something going on if you were sneaking around our basement." Yume glanced up at Zane as he lowered his head and took in a deep breath before looking back up at Diana.

"We are here because we need your assistance," he replied, "our worlds are both on the verge of destruction." His unwavering gaze never left hers, and he continued. "Your father foresaw that a great evil would descend on our world. If that were to happen, it would throw off the balance of our worlds. We have been charged with bringing you back to the dream world with us."

"Unbalanced how?"

"Sandmen have begun to go missing, which affects the ability to deliver dream sand to your world. People need dreams to be able to process their subconscious thoughts. When people can't dream, and the balance is thrown, you can see it manifest in destructive ways. People become easily angered and rude, creating an increase in episodes of violence.

Diana thought about the fights on the news and the road rage with the lady and her cane. Even the rude people at the volleyball game. *Could this all be related?*

"What can I possibly do, and how come if my father needs me, why didn't he come here himself?" she asked.

"He's missing," Yume chimed in, in a tone that was perhaps a bit too chipper for that particular news. Diana was shocked to hear Yume speak. Zane turned and flashed a stern look at Yume, who seemed unfazed by it. Yume looked back at Zane as she crossed the room and hopped on the bed to get comfortable.

"He's missing," Diana asked, "what happened to him?" Zane glared at Yume and sighed, turning back to Diana.

"His whereabouts are currently unknown, but we don't know that any horrific acts are to blame. Warrick has been known to go off on his own for long periods of time. He was aware of the missing sandmen when he went off to inspect the castle and prepare for your arrival."

"He told us to come get you if he wasn't back in two weeks, and now, we're here," Yume interjected as she rolled around on the bed to make herself comfortable. Apparently, not as concerned by the situation as Zane was.

"He was here," Selene said, speaking up. Everyone turned to look at her, the shock on their faces palpable. Even Yume was now at full attention, awaiting what Selene would say next.

"He was here, in our house," Diana stammered, "when was this?"

"A few nights ago, he was here, Selene said, "he came to let me know the danger he foresaw was finally beginning to manifest itself, and despite his best efforts, you were going to be brought into the fray. He brought several items he thought would help you to best whatever was causing the great unbalance in the worlds. He also needed to contact people I work with and did not want to draw much attention to it."

The shock and hurt shot through Diana's body. Her father had been here. After all this time, he had been so close.

"But Mom, you're a maid. I can't imagine that sloppy beds and dirty toilets could be destroying the balance of the worlds," she said, harsher than intended.

Diana saw the hurt on her mother's face, immediately regretting her tone.

"Well, actually, that's not the kind of maid that I am sweetheart," Selene explained. "The hotel I work for in the city is actually a magical hub in this world. It's home to many magical creatures and witches. Our job as maids is to clean up magical messes and accidents in order to keep our secret hidden away from those who might fear or cause us harm. The safety of magical people in this realm is dependent on the maid service. That's also how I knew that I needed to return home to you, I cast wards around the house to alert me to magic being used. Warrick told me that Zane and Yume would be here to take you with them, and in this way, I was prepared. When my wards were activated this evening, I rippled home as quick as I could."

All Diana could do was stand there. Yet another piece of what she thought she knew about her life was stripped away. Sandmen, witches, baku, magic hotels, lost fathers, magic spells, and worlds in danger. All in all, Diana thought she was handling it all in stride. She had no idea what the next reveal could possibly be.

"Where are the items that Warrick left for Diana?" Zane asked. "I assume you took proper precautions with them."

"Of course," Selene replied with a hint of offense in her voice, "protecting magic is what I do for a living. You'd be hard-pressed to find someone better to protect them." She gave a self-congratulating hair flip while standing assertively.

"Where did you put them?" Yume asked, jumping off the bed excitedly. "Is it at the hotel? Can we go?"

"It's actually in the basement," Selene said. Yume's tail sagged, not able to hide her disappointment.

"Perhaps we should retrieve them," Zane said.

"Absolutely. Are you ready, Diana?" Selene asked.

"Ready as I'll ever be," she replied, heading towards the door following her mother. She wondered what more could be waiting for her in the basement.

FIVE

Selene led the way down the hall to the stairs. They made their way downstairs with Yume floating behind them, walking on air with purple tufts of smoke trailing from her feet. The group passed through the kitchen and down to the basement. Selene led them past the living space and through the door to the storage area, up to the far wall.

"Alright, this is it," Selene said.

She positioned her body in front of the wall. She raised her hands high above her head, with only her index fingers extended. She touched her index fingers together, and then, with a sharp, quick motion, she pulled her arms apart and down.

A green light emitted from the wall in the shape of a door. She crossed her arms with her index and middle fingers out and then circled her arms out in a clockwise motion till they were back where they began the motion. She drew her hands back to her center, palms out. She took a moment to focus as green energy formed in her outmost hand. She thrust her hands out, and the energy hit the center of the glowing doorway.

The energy flowed out from the center, like a diluted gel, until the whole thing glowed green. Selene slowly wiggled her fingers and pulled her hands slightly apart. The green light began to billow, transforming into luxurious velvet curtains. The curtains parted, revealing a large room equal in size to the rest of the basement.

Diana was overcome with a sense of wonder and awe as she processed what she had just witnessed. She had never seen anything like it before. Her mother's magic was beautiful to behold, but that was only the tip of the iceberg.

Diana stepped inside the hidden room. It was nothing like she would have expected. It was laid out like a super posh sitting room that you would see on the home design channel. The walls were lined with shelves and cabinets filled with books and potion ingredients. Plush velvet drapes hung down the walls between the shelves and cabinetry. There were couches and chairs upholstered in a similar green fabric to that of the curtains that formed to let them in. The center of the room housed a large altar with candles and stones with a cauldron prominently featured in the middle. A scent of cinnamon incense filled the room, emanating from the blazing fireplace at the far side of the room.

The rest of the group filed into the room. Yume's face lit up, and she bound over to one of the couches and made herself at home. Zane looked over the room. If he was at all impressed, his face gave no clues to it. Selene's face was practically glowing. Her smile filled her face, showing the pride that she took in the space and the joy she had in being able to share it.

Selene walked over to a cabinet and waved her hand over it. The cabinet opened, revealing a box covered with tiny purple crystal shards. With a wave of her hand, Selene sent the box hovering across the room to a table near the fire.

"Diana, come have a look," Selene said. Diana approached the box with apprehension. She had no idea what could be waiting for her inside the box. She reached for the box. Her lips pursed to the side, and her brow crinkled. She couldn't figure out how to open it. She tried to pull on the lid, but it wouldn't budge.

"I think it's stuck," Diana said.

"Oh, of course, you need magic to open the box," Selene said.

"Well, don't I have magic?"

"Warrick was worried that the forces that were going to move against the dream world would be able to sense your sandman magic. Unfortunately, to keep you safe and protected, I had to bind your powers when you were young." Selene made a gesture with her hand. A drawer in a cabinet opened, and a bottle floated over. Yume batted at it with her trunk and giggled. Selene plucked the floating vial out of the air and turned back to Diana. "This potion will release the magic that is bound inside you. Once you drink this, all your power will return. It's going to be very intense as years of power return all at once." She looked into her daughter's eyes intently. "There is no going back once you take the potion, your life will never be the same."

There was so much to take in. Diana didn't know how to process it all. Unleashing her latent magic would be connecting to an entirely new part of herself and her family. While it also has the potential to lead a potentially world-shifting dangerous force directly to her. A force that they wanted her to help vanquish. The pluses and minuses kept playing through her mind. How could Diana make such an impossible large decision?

"Do you think I can handle it?" Diana asked, her stomach in knots.

"Magic is a blessing that is only given to those who can handle it," Selene replied, smiling at her daughter. "You are innately magically you were meant to have magic, it's part of your destiny and makes you who you are. That's not to say that there won't be an adjustment or that it will all come easily."

Diana reached for the vial and examined the liquid inside. It was sparkly and blue in color. She thought that this must be what unicorn tears would look like. She swirled the liquid around. It was a thick consistency that was slow-moving, like syrup. The more she swirled it, the more it started to glow. As she held the vial, she could feel its energy radiating out from it, tingling up her arm. The sensation was similar to what she had felt on the beach earlier. That powerful, connected feeling. She tightened her fist around the bottle and looked back up at everyone. They were all staring at her, waiting to see what she was going to do. She wasn't sure what exactly was in store for her. But the gnawing thoughts about improving her family bonds wouldn't leave her mind. She knew what she had to do.

"I'm ready," Diana said. Everyone looked pleased except Zane. He looked rather indifferent, as seemed to be his style, but he wasn't breaking his gaze from her.

"Alright," Selene said, "perhaps you should come over and sit on one of the couches, this could be really intense."

Selene took her daughter's hand and led her over to the couch opposite the one that Yume was occupying. Diana sat down and looked at everyone watching her. She took a deep breath. Her heartbeat quickened. Her hands were shaking. She removed the stopper from the vial, and the earthy scent of frankincense filled her nose. Then, in one fluid motion, she drank the potion.

A rush hit her like a tidal wave as the bitter potion worked its way down. Energy washed over her entire body, unlike anything she had ever experienced. It was so intense that she couldn't see anything beyond a kaleidoscope of swirling colors. It was as if she was floating in a rainbow bubble. The warm energy continued to flow and pulse beyond herself, making her dizzy.

Diana felt the heartbeats of the others in the room as her own heart raced. Her energy continued to reach out and mingle with the others in the room, allowing her to sense anticipation from everyone. The swirling energy began to contract from the room and focus in on her body. The swirling intensified like water rushing down a drain. The colors in her vision flashed brightly. Then, with a final rush, the energy settled, and Diana collapsed on the couch.

Diana batted her eyes as she began to come to. She slowly sat herself, trying to stop the room from spinning. As her vision cleared, she saw Selene sitting next to her on the couch. She rubbed her eyes as she felt a headache forming from the head rush. Other than that, she felt good. There was something different about how Diana felt, but she couldn't quite put it into thoughts or words.

"How do you feel?" Selene asked

"Different, but a good different."

"Do you need a minute," Selene said, reading the strain on her daughter's face, "I know that was a lot to take in."

"No, I think I'm fine, "she said, standing up shakily. Knowing if she didn't continue right away, she never would. "Let's see what's in the box."

Selene helped Diana over to where the box was waiting. Yume followed along as well, giving up the comfort of the couch to the intrigue of the box. Zane also followed, standing slightly behind. Instinctively, Diana reached out for the box. She ran her finger over a larger shard on the top of the box. A spark zapped her finger like static electricity. The shard began to glow, with the other shards on the box following suit. The glowing faded, and the lid to the box opened to reveal its contents.

Diana began to pull the items out of the box and look them over. The first thing she pulled out was a dream catcher. It had purple beads that appeared to match the shards on the box, strung among the exquisitely intricate weaving. Long, beautiful feathers caught the light. Shimmering as they hung down from the catcher. It was a type of feather that she couldn't identify.

The next item she found was a key. It was a skeleton key made from the same purple crystal and had a small yellow shard on it. She ran her fingers over the ornate carvings that ran across its surface.

She continued to explore the contents of the box and pulled out a drawstring pouch. It looked familiar, she glanced over at Zane and saw a similar pouch hanging by his hip. She opened it up and reached inside. It was full of purple-hued sand. She let it run through her fingers. There was an energy about the sand. It felt like potential, for lack of a better word.

At the bottom of the box, neatly folded, was a set of robes also similar in style to Zane's. The linens felt strong yet soft to the touch.

Diana wasn't sure what it all meant or how it was all used, but she could feel emotions rising in her like the tide. These were all things left by a father she had never known, one who, apparently, was now missing. Looking the items over, something in the box caught her eye. It had been covered by the robes, so she had missed it.

She pulled back the robes to reveal a photograph. Diana picked it up and looked at the image facing her; she was unable to stop the tears from rolling down her face. Selene saw her daughter's tears.

"What's wrong?" Selene asked.

"Nothing," she said as she began to smile through her tears.

Looking up at her was a happy, smiling family. There was what must have been a twenty-one-year-old Selene looking up at her. Diana saw herself as a baby laughing and giggling and being held by a man she didn't immediately recognize but knew he must be her father. His purple eyes looked up at her, and it was like looking at her own. His white hair and beard were neat and orderly and contrasted by the deep tan of his skin. He appeared to be slightly older than her mother; then, something clicked in her mind. *Could this be the man from the fireplace?* She couldn't stop crying. In her hands, she held the thing she had always wanted. A happy family. Her emotions were beginning to overwhelm her. She never wanted to stop looking at this picture.

"Please excuse me for a moment," she said as she ran from the room and upstairs. Diana stepped out into her backyard and took a seat on the side of the deck. She looked at the picture again. She tried to process everything she was feeling. There was a mix of sadness and anger that ebbed and flowed within her. Here, in her hand, was a photo of what she always wanted. A dream beyond her reach, but literally in her grasp.

Why did her father leave and never visit her again? Why did her mother spend all her time away at work? Why wasn't this family enough for them? Why wasn't she enough for them?

The backdoor opened, and she wiped away her tears and turned, expecting to see her mother. She was shocked to see Zane walking towards her. He stood beside her, not looking at her instead, he gazed at the full moon. His purple eyes sparkled in the moonlight. Diana looked up at his solemn face.

"There is much you have learned tonight," he said finally, "and there is still much for you to learn. Whole new worlds are now literally open to you. Now you have to decide what you want to do; no one will make that choice for you." He paused, never breaking his gaze from the moon. "We really do need your help, and hopefully, we can count on you."

Zane turned and looked Diana directly into her eyes. Diana pulled back due to his intensity, but she met his gaze and could read a hint of sadness in his eyes and felt herself relax. Zane recomposed himself and headed back into the house.

Diana took a few more minutes to gather her thoughts and center herself. She stood up, looking up once more at the moon. Diana could feel its energy encompassing her like a warm blanket. She let out a deep breath through her pursed lips, knowing what she had to do, and walked back into the house.

As she entered the secret chamber in the basement, she found everyone was waiting for her. No one said anything as she made her way towards them. She reached the center of the room where her mother and Yume were waiting on opposite couches while Zane was hanging back against a bookshelf. Diana looked at the expressions on their faces. There was a mix of anticipation, hope, and worry.

"I've made a decision," she said. "While I'm not exactly sure what I can do or what we are up against. If there is a possibility that I can help, even if I'm not sure how. I need to do it. I want to help locate my father and finally meet him. I want to know more about who I am and where I come from."

Yume leapt from the couch and gleefully bounded over to Diana.

Selene stood up and somberly made her way over to Diana. Her face was a mix of pride and despair. Tears began to roll down her face as she pulled her daughter into a hug.

"I always knew this day would come, and I've dreaded it for as long as I can remember," she said as she pulled back to look at her daughter, "I've been a terrible mother. I always thought that if I was to distance myself, it would make this day easier for both of us. I thought it would hurt me less if you left and that there would be less to hold you back from who you were meant to be. I know how wrong I was and how much hurt I've caused you. There is nothing I can do to erase that, but hopefully, going forward, we can rebuild our relationship." She stepped back, wiping away her tears.

Diana put her hands over her heart. Hearing her mother's words, feeling the pain that she had also been struggling. Diana felt closer to her mother than she ever had.

Selene walked over to a cabinet and pulled out another box. This box was less ornate than the one from Diana's father but did have some beautiful details in the wood. She placed the box beside the other and motioned for Diana to come over.

Diana walked back over to where the boxes were waiting for her.

"This one is from me," Selene said, stepping aside to make room for Diana.

She ran her fingers over the box that her mother had presented. The wood was smooth and warm. As she traced the designs with her finger, she could feel the energy that was concealed within it. She tried to lift the latch, but it wouldn't budge. She noticed the small jewel that was on the latch. She tapped it and felt a spark as her magic released the latch, and the top flipped open.

Diana reached in and pulled out a tiny book bound in purple leather with several ribbon bookmarks dangling down from between the pages. She flipped through the pages and discovered that it contained handwritten spells and magical know-how.

Next, she pulled out a wand that appeared to be made of the same wood as the box. The carvings on the box even matched the markings on the handle of the wand. She held the wand in front of her and waved it gracefully through the air. The tip of the wand glowed as its energy synced with hers.

The final item in the box was a simple yet beautiful ring of silver that had a tiny crystal orb, about the size of a pea, set on top.

"This wand was my very first wand," Selene said, "It's been passed down through our family for generations." Selene picked up the book. "I wrote this spell book for you with many simple beginner spells that every witch should know, along with others that are a bit more advanced but may come in handy for your journey. I put the bookmarks at the particularly helpful spells that you might need." She then took the ring and slid it on the index finger of Diana's left hand. "This crystal ball ring is always worn on one's receptive hand, whereas wands are held in your projective hand to help amplify your magic. The crystal ball can help reveal more than is easily seen." Selene waved a hand over the ring, and the crystal grew until it was as wide as a quarter. "When you activate the ring, you can gaze into it and see more clearly into a situation." Then, with a swirl of her finger, Selene returned the jewel to its original size.

Selene held Diana's hands. "I wish I could go with to help you, but only those born of the dream world may enter."

"Thank you, Mom," Diana said, "these will be very helpful."

Diana gave her mother an extra-long hug, not wanting to let go. She finally released the embrace and turned to Zane and Yume.

"Well, I guess it's about time to head out," she said nervously.

"Just one more thing," Selene said, and with a grand gesture, all the items in the boxes swirled away in a trail of smoke that encircled Diana. As the smoke cleared, Diana was fully dressed in her sandman robes. The robes were tossed around her in a casual, flowing manner. The sand pouch was attached at her hip, and the other items were stashed away in hidden pockets.

Diana put up her hood. Standing there in her robes, she felt confident in a way she had never felt before. She felt like she was somewhat ready to go on this crazy journey. It was a tremendous feeling. She saw everyone looking at her, and just for a moment, she thought she saw a glimmer of a smile break the normally stoic face of Zane.

"It's time," Zane said. Diana gave her mother one last hug before joining Zane and Yume in the center of the room. Zane took Diana's hand in his while Yume floated on his other side. He looked Diana in the eye with the most reassuring look on his face. The group began to be surrounded by particles that shone with the light of the moon. It swirled faster and faster. The brightness intensified until, with a flash, a vacancy was revealed where the three of them had stood. Leaving Selene alone in the secret chamber.

SIX

Diana's eyes were blinded by swirling light. It was as if a million tiny flashbulbs were going off all around her. Diana's body rose into the air. Her toes dangling just above the ground. The world around her began to swirl away. Totally disoriented, up and down had no meaning. Her stomach lurched, and just as she was going to be ill, the sensation of being pulled through a drain overcame her. The swirling intensified as the light shined with renewed intensity. The pulling forces abruptly stopped, and Diana fell to the ground as the light dissipated.

Zane reached down, helping her to her feet. Diana dusted herself off and began to take in her surroundings.

The sight before her eyes was breathtaking. She stood on a beach that sat on the edge of an endless ocean. The twinkling stars reflected over the water, creating an endless tapestry. It was impossible to tell where the water ended and the night sky began. Behind her was a large cliff side of glowing amethyst that towered above her. The most incredible sight, however, was the several moons that lined the starry sky. Hanging like iridescent pearls. One was familiar. It looked just as the moon did back home. The others, however, were all slightly different in color and surface texture.

"Welcome to Sabnare," Zane said.

"Isn't it wonderful," Yume chimed in, floating about.

"Sabnare . . ." Diana said, letting the name of the dream world trail off as she took it all in.

"Let's go," Zane said as he started to walk down the beach, "we have much to do." Diana hurried to keep up while Yume kept pace, floating lazily behind.

Making their way down the beach, a subtle breeze came off of the ocean. It gently swirled the leaves of an odd-looking palm tree, leaving the scent of lavender in the air. The trunks were the size and shape of regular palms, but their bark was like that of a birch tree. Its peeling white bark mirroring the gentle glow of the moons above. The traditional-looking palm leaves were purple in color and shot out from bunches of purple flowers at the top of the trunk.

As they continued down the beach, following the natural curve of the mountains and the coastline, a village began to enter their sight. The village was comprised of what looked like Middle Eastern adobe-style buildings. They were a mix of single and multilevel buildings. The base structures were box-like, with many different stacking combinations. Diana could see awnings made from a silky translucent material on many of the buildings. Plants were plentiful. Flowers and herbs were being grown in window boxes as well as on rooftops. The buildings had exposed wooden beams that protruded out of the stone sides.

The group reached the edge of the village. Zane turned to look at Diana.

"Be sure to keep yourself covered," He said, looking over the path ahead, "we don't want to draw attention to you."

Diana adjusted her robes and pulled the hood farther to the front to shelter her face. Yume landed beside her and trotted along as they headed into the village. As they walked down the main strip in the center of town, Diana felt a sense of calm. The village had a relaxed pace. From beneath her hood, she watched sandmen leisurely make their way down the streets. Stopping to chat with others. She also noticed that Zane's pace had also slowed down significantly. The fast stride that brought them to the village was no more.

Walking towards them on the opposite side of the path was a group of three baku. The appearance of the baku intrigued Diana, whereas the tapirs they resembled had a mostly uniform look. Baku's appearance varied greatly by color, size, and form. One looked similar in size and appearance to Yume but in shades of teal and yellow. The others were larger with long, pronounced tusks. One was black and red and had a mane that appeared to be made of a shimmering yellow smoke. The other was purple, with orange leopard-like spots.

As the other baku passed, Diana noticed the slightest motion. The large tusked baku with the mane glanced out of the corner of his eye. He shifted his weight. Smack! One turn of his head and his tusk struck Yume from behind. Yume fell face-first into the sand. The baku began to laugh as they continued on their way.

Diana turned to confront them.

"Hey…" she began to say until Zane grabbed her arm and turned her back around.

"We can't draw attention to you." He said forcefully.

Yume turned her head down and away and continued to walk. Diana's stomach was turning. Yume's naturally upbeat and joyful nature seemed to be completely gone. In her place was a melancholy doppelgänger. Diana didn't know what to say. She reached down and cupped Yume's trunk in her hand. Yume looked up at Diana. Diana gave her trunk a light, reassuring squeeze. Yume began to smile, and they continued walking, trunk in hand.

Zane continued to lead them through the twists and turns of the village's streets. Finally, they approached a building slightly outside the village. It was sitting on its own, nestled cozily among a group of lavender palms partially obscured by the mountainside, it appeared to be coming out of the mountain itself.

"This is your father's home," Zane said.

He pulled out a key that appeared to be nearly identical to the one Diana had received from her father. She reached into her pouch and retrieved the key.

"Is this key for his house?" Diana asked, holding it up.

"It's much more than just a simple door key," he explained. "It's imbued with great magic."

Diana looked at the wooden door in front of her. There was no keyhole. Zane noticed the puzzled look on her face.

"Here," he said, moving over to the door, "like this."

Zane, with the key firmly in hand, extended his arm so that the tip of the key touched the door. He turned the key a quarter turn to the left in a clean, sharp motion. A burst of purple light quickly lit the door. In a single fluid motion, it melted from the top down into translucent drapes. They were just like the ones she had seen in the village. As they stepped through the doorway, Zane turned back to the curtains. With an equally sharp motion as before, he reached out with the key and made a quarter turn to the right. A flash lit up the curtains as they began to solidify. As it turned back into wood, it reminded Diana of a tree growing out of the ground.

Diana turned to face the room. Yume happily hopped over to a pillow in the corner of the room near a crackling fireplace that filled the room with the scent of sandalwood. A large, cluttered desk sat at the back of the room, flanked by bookshelves on either side of it. The shelves were overflowing with scrolls, books, and a plethora of other items. Opposite the fireplace hung an ornate wall tapestry depicting a dragon bathed in moonlight. Similar to the one in her dream that hung by the fire. Diana turned back towards the door and saw a table to one side that had several statues of bipedal cats, and to the other side of the door sat a large diamond-encrusted chest.

Zane made his way to the center of the room near an oversized plush sofa. He motioned towards the doorways on either side of the hanging tapestry.

"The kitchen and bedroom are over here," Zane said, "make

yourself at home." He returned his gaze to Diana. "I need to run out for a moment to prepare the next steps that Warrick set in place now that you're here. Yume will stay with you while I'm gone." He glanced at Yume, "Yume, please take care of Diana while I'm away."

Yume glided over to Diana's side, "Of course, Zane! Nothing to worry about here. Diana and I will be just fine."

Zane left quickly, locking up behind him. Leaving Diana and Yume on their own.

Diana and Yume headed into the kitchen. Diana felt as if she had stepped back in time. The kitchen had no modern appliances. There was a sink and counters and an old wood-burning stove. Diana filled a kettle with water and let it begin to heat up on the stove.

"Yume, would you like some tea?"

"No, none for me, thanks!"

She searched through the first set of cabinets and found several glass jars of loose-leaf tea. She took out a jar of valerian root tea and set it on the counter while she rummaged through the drawers for a tea infuser. She filled it with the tea and began to look for a cup in the cabinets.

When she opened the one that was filled with glasses, one mug stood out among the others. Diana smiled as she looked at a familiar sight. She pulled it down and took a closer look at the scene being played out on the mug. It featured cartoon cows grazing in a field on a sunny day. It was as if it came out of her mother's own collection.

"That's your dad's favorite mug," Yume chirped in excitedly, "he's always drinking from that one."

Diana's heart felt full, seeing such a sweet connection between her parents. She finished making her tea and returned to the main room, settling in on the couch next to Yume.

"So," Diana said tentatively, "what was up with those other baku?"

"I've never really been accepted fully by the herd," Yume fidgeted with her trunk. "When I was just a baby, I was found on my own, separated from the rest of the herd by Warrick, he took me in and took care of me. He searched for my parents but wasn't able to find out what happened to them. The rest of the herd was distrusting of Warrick because baku had never just disappeared before. Baku and sandmen have always had a civil relationship, but they mostly do their own thing. So, as I grew older and remained close to Warrick, it drove a wedge between myself and many members of the herd."

"I'm so sorry, Yume, that must be difficult."

"No worries," she said, as a smile returned to her face. "Overall, I'm very happy and focused on the wonderful things and people in my life."

"I wish I had your optimism," Diana sighed. "Even now, I feel out of my depth, and I have no idea what I'm supposed to do to protect this place."

"If there is one thing I know, it's to trust Warrick's judgment. He believes in you, and you are his daughter, so his greatness is in you as well."

"I just don't want to let anyone down."

"You won't. You are literally in a world of dreams, and you are a part of that world. Dreams are about potential and what could be. All the potential of Sabnare runs through you."

Diana leaned in and hugged Yume. Yume's body relaxed in her arms, and she placed her trunk over the back of Diana's neck. They released from the embrace, and Diana took a sip of her tea.

"How about we go through some of these papers to try and see if we can figure out where my father went," she said, walking over to the desk with Yume at her side.

Diana started going through the numerous scrolls and papers on the desk while Yume worked on a nearby bookshelf. There was so much information to take in and things that made little to no sense to her. She came across phrases like forty wynx, The Fracture, and sandmages. Diana turned, knocking a bunch of papers and scrolls to the floor. She gathered them up while trying to keep some sort of order and placed the papers and scrolls on the desk. One scroll stood out, being much more ornate with its metal casing. Before she could inspect it further, Yume called out to her.

"Diana, look what I found," Yume said, holding up a leather-bound book with her trunk. "I can't get it to open; maybe you should try."

Yume handed the book over to Diana. She tried to open the book, but it was like one solid block, even though she could see the pages. She inspected the cover more closely and saw a purple crystal shard on the cover. Diana ran a finger over it. A gentle wave of pale red energy rippled out from the shard until it had passed over the whole book and then dissipated. She tried the cover again and opened it with ease.

"Blood lock!" Yume chirped.

"What's a blood lock?"

"It's a way magical beings seal away their most important secrets. It makes it impossible for anyone not related by blood to gain access to certain places or objects."

"Whatever is in here must be valuable information. Were there any others like this?"

"No, none of the other books I found were sealed."

Diana began flipping through the pages. The anticipation made her arms break out in goosebumps. An envelope fell out and glided to the ground as she flipped through the pages. Diana and Yume turned to see what it was. Scrawled out on the envelope was a single word: Diana. She moved over to the couch, her legs weak upon seeing her name. Her hands quivered as she opened the envelope, retrieving the letter from inside.

Diana,

I hoped this day would never come. I did all I could to prevent the events that brought you here. All I ever wanted was your happiness. Unfortunately, I was not able to protect you. I wish I could be there in person to help guide you. The scroll on the desk contains as much information on Sabnare as I could gather. Let it, and my love, guide you as you face your destiny.

Diana smiled, wiping a tear from her eye. "Yume, can you bring me the scroll that's sitting on the desk?"

Yume hovered over, grabbing the scroll in her trunk, and floated over to the couch in a swirl of sparkly smoke.

"Thank you," Diana said, taking the scroll from Yume.

The scroll was encased in an exquisitely decorated gold cover. Encrusted with the familiar purple crystals of Sabnare. The sides of the scroll had what appeared to be little bat wings. The magical energy of the scroll beat like a heart, passing through her body as she held it in her hands. The front of the casing had a large seal on its front. Diana traced her finger across it.

A red aura emanated from the seal as it began to glow. The pulsating energy rippled out in scarlet waves surrounding the scroll. The wings on the side sprang to life, vigorously flapping, lifting the scroll out of Diana's hands. The red energy faded as the seal began to shine with radiant purple energy, swirling around the scroll lazily.

Diana reached out and gently touched the seal. The light pulsed, and the scroll began to open like a projector screen. The seal's light faded away as the parchment was bathed in light that mirrored the glow of the moon. Diana watched intently as a photorealistic image appeared on the page.

"That's Sabnare," Yume said, hovering by Diana's side.

The island of Sabnare was beautiful. The mountains of amethyst almost completely encircled the island, except for a small opening near where the village stood. A large river valley ran through the surrounding mountains. In the center of the island was a large desert.

"Is there anything in the desert?" Diana asked while casually swiping her hand towards the center of the island. The image of

Sabnare faded away, and new images appeared much like windows on a computer. She began scrolling through the images that appeared on the scroll as if browsing on a tablet. *How Cool.* The sight of a large sandcastle caught her eye.

"That's the main headquarters of the sandmen," Yume explained, "that is where the higher-ranking sandmen live and work. Those who collect and deliver the dream sand, along with the elders who watch over and run Sabnare, are some of the people you'll find there."

"I'd love to see it," Diana said, taking it all in. Yume shifted uncomfortably. She gently sank into the couch and averted her gaze.

"Yume, what is it?" Diana asked. Yume turned to look her in the eye.

"I'm not really sure how well you'd be received."

"Why do you say that?"

"There are no sandmen that are women. They are seen as inferior."

"Wait, what?" Diana stammered.

"All I know is that centuries ago, there used to be female sandmen. Something happened, and now they are no longer allowed to be sandmen, not that there were many in the first place. That's why Zane wanted you to keep covered in the village."

Diana was stunned at what she had just heard. *How could this possibly be true?* She crossed her arms and began rubbing her upper arms, trying to process what that meant for her, as apparently the only female sandman.

"Any idea on what happened to make them feel that way?" she asked Yume.

"Sandmen hold their history close, so close in fact that I doubt many sandmen know exactly why things are the way they are. They just march on with tradition and do their job."

The familiar sensation of self-doubt came spiraling in. How could she do everything she was supposed to do? Did anyone else even want her here? Was her presence going to cause problems? A touch brought her back, out of her head space. It was Yume's trunk resting on her shoulder.

"Don't overthink it," Yume said, "I shouldn't have said anything, it's been so long since this has even been an issue." Diana could feel the compassion in Yume's eyes. Seeing her smile and the softness in the caress of her trunk, Diana began to once again feel at ease. There was a purity in Yume that made the idea of everything that has happened and was yet to happen a little easier to digest.

Diana and Yume continued looking over the scroll, swiping through images and words. They were lost in the process when a sound at the door brought them back. The door faded from wood into curtains as Zane entered. Zane quickly returned the door into its locked, wooden form. Diana got up from the couch, with Yume right behind her, and walked over to where Zane was standing.

"Welcome back," Diana said.

"Thank you. Did you both get on alright while I was away?" Zane replied.

"We sure did," Yume chirped.

"Good," Zane turned to Diana, "It's time to begin your training as a sandman." He looked at Yume, "You stay here, and we will be back."

"Sure thing," Yume replied.

"Are you ready?" he asked Diana.

Diana looked down, took a deep breath, and centered herself. The beating of her heart was almost deafening. She bit her bottom lip and looked up at Zane.

"As I'll ever be."

Zane and Diana left Warrick's, following the curve of the luminescent mountains while the brilliant glow of the moons lit their way. They reached a small pond that formed where water trickled out of the side of the amethyst mountain. Several baku were lying near the water, extending their trunks to smell the blue lotus flowers that bloomed there. Beyond the pond stood a large stone building reminiscent of the Roman Colosseum.

"That's the academy," Zane stated while looking across the water. "That is where all new sandmen go to learn how to use their powers." He paused and turned his head to look at Diana. "And now that I've arranged for you to have private training, you will be a part of that legacy."

Diana turned to meet his eyes, and he turned away. His solemn face transfixed on the academy. Zane stood tall and rigid, lost in his thoughts.

"We should continue," he said, not breaking his gaze and resuming his walk around the pond. Diana quickly followed behind.

They had just about reached the tip of the pond when a voice called out.

"Zane!"

Diana and Zane turned to see where the voice had come from. A sharp, silent gasp filled her lungs. It was a sight unlike anything she'd seen. A robed figure was swiftly gliding over the sand in their direction.

"Keep covered," Zane reminded Diana. She adjusted her robes and pulled her hood forward, obscuring her face.

The other sandman closed the distance between them, his hooded wrap falling back as he turned into a stop like an Olympic skier. Diana looked over the new sandman standing before them. He appeared to be slightly younger than Zane, with deep violet eyes shining in the moonlight. His hair was much like that of Zane's, white but short and spiked. His smooth, androgynous features made him look as if a faerie had appeared before her. Zane was the first to speak.

"Hello Phelipe."

"Hey Zane," he said cheerfully, "I have some really big news!"

Zane silently waited for Phelipe to continue. Diana kept her head down and away from Phelipe's view.

"I just received a messenger bat summoning me to the castle," he continued, "I'm finally moving up to be a full-fledged Dream Duster. I would have been fine with being a Sand Keeper or even a Dream Keeper, but I'm so excited I get to be a Dream Duster!"

Diana shuffled uncomfortably while Phelipe continued his excited ramblings. Zane's normally stoic face was beginning to crack with exasperation. Zane reached out and took Diana's hand, and interrupted Phelipe.

"Congratulations, Phelipe. I know how much you've wanted this, but we have to get going now."

"Oh, okay, I have to be on my way as well," he said. Phelipe turned to notice Diana for the first time and reached out his hand.

"Hi, I'm sorry I never introduced myself, I'm Phelipe."

Diana reached out her hand and shook his, never revealing her face to him, quickly recoiling her hand back into her robes. Zane began to head toward the academy while still holding onto her other hand.

"I didn't catch your name," Phelipe prodded, as one eyebrow raised.

"Sorry, but we have to go," Zane said sternly, never breaking his stride.

"Oh, alright, see you later, nice to meet you," Phelipe called out, his face twisting into a mischievous grin.

With a motion of his hand, a bit of sand jumped up and knocked Diana's hood back. Revealing her hair. Then, with a twist of his finger, the sand beneath Diana turned, spinning her around, forcing her to fall backward and land in the sand. Phelipe laughed and made a pulling motion towards himself, forcing the sand to send Diana directly to him. He reached out his hand and helped her back to her feet. Diana began to brush all the sand off.

"Let me get that," Phelipe said, and with a downwards flourish of his hands, the sand released itself from her robes. "So, what do we have here?" he said inquisitively. He could barely contain the excitement on his face. A smile spread from ear to ear, and his eyes opened wide enough for the moons to be reflected in them.

"This is Diana," Zane said, "Warrick's daughter." Phelipe arched his eyebrows and tilted his head.

"You don't say," Phelipe replied cheekily, looking her over. "Are you a genie?"

"I'm a sandman," Diana replied, confused. "Well, half sandman."

"Half sandman, half what?" he probed.

"Half human," she started, "well, my mom's a witch, so I guess actually, half witch."

"Zane, is this true?"

"Yes, it's just as she says," Zane stated.

"She's not a genie?" Phelipe stood there, hands on his hips and a confused look on his face. He looked Diana up and down, taking everything in.

Zane quickly glanced at Diana and back at Phelipe before responding. "She's not a genie."

"Does Malvin know about her?" Phelipe asked nervously.

Zane's normally calm, expressionless face had changed. His eyes became hyper-focused, and his body rigid. Diana had never seen him look more serious.

"Phelipe, I need you to promise me that you won't say a word to Malvin about Diana," he said, staring daggers. "If you do, she won't be able to fulfill her duties, and many people could be in danger. Warrick warned us of a great evil that would come to Sabnare and that Diana is the only one who can stop it. We know that some sandmen have gone missing, and we are trying to figure everything out."

Phelipe got quiet and stood up straight. Gone was the Joker, and in his place stood a man of seriousness and sincerity. He looked at Diana and smiled, and returned his focus to Zane.

"You have my word, I know how intense Malvin can be," he said.

Zane let out a sigh as his muscles loosened, relaxing his body, and a calm spread across his face.

"Thank you," he said, "now we really must be going, but do be careful."

"I will, and I should head to the castle anyway." He turned to Diana, "It was a pleasure to meet you." Phelipe gave her a warm hug. He flashed a smile that matched his personality of sunshine in a land of endless night. He then looked back at Zane, "See you around."

Phelipe closed his eyes and lowered his head. His body began to glow as he was surrounded by glowing orbs of moonlight. Lifting his head, the lights swirled faster, and with one final flash, he was gone.

Diana stood there, staring at the spot where Phelipe had stood. Zane's neutral expression had returned, and he began heading back towards the academy. Diana quickly matched his pace.

"Why did he think I might be a genie?" Diana asked as they walked.

"Because there are no female sandmen," he replied. "Anytime a female sandman comes into existence, they are turned into genies."

"Why would they do that?"

"No one is certain when it started, but it's been this way for as long as anybody can remember," he said. "It's said that originally, there were female sandmen as well, but they took a more active role in dispensing dreams. Many would try to impart nothing but good dreams."

"Well, that doesn't sound like a bad thing."

"Their intentions were pure, but humans need to be able to process their subconscious thoughts as they dream so they can better handle their hopes and fears in the waking hours. Even nightmares, as terrifying as they can sometimes be, allow people to confront things they need to work through."

"I guess that makes sense," she said reflectively.

"There was also the matter of dream diving."

"What's dream diving?"

"Dream diving is an ability sandmen have that allows you to enter the dreams of another person. Dream diving is seen as an invasion of privacy in most cases. Sandmen are supposed to be passive in their work. You help people fall asleep, deliver dreams, and that's it."

"Oh, wow, I had no idea."

"They say that one female sandman was flagrantly disobeying the rules. That she saw no harm in giving people what they wanted in their dreams. So, the council decided that would be her punishment; she would give people everything they wanted at the cost of her freedom. So, she was locked away in a bottle and became the first genie. She had many followers who believed as she did, and as they spoke out in her favor, they suffered the same fate. The council made a far-reaching judgment that all future female sandmen would be genies and tend to the wishes of humankind."

There was so much for Diana to process about this new world she had been thrust into. She never expected that the world of dreams could be so complicated, but Sabnare was proving to be just that. Before she could think about it any longer, they arrived at the front door of the academy. Zane looked at Diana.

"Are you ready to take the next step in becoming who you truly are?" Zane asked.

Diana breathed deeply, filling her lungs with the clean Sabnare air. She released her breath and, with it, the self-doubt that liked to creep in. With her head held high, she stared at the door that stood before her. The threshold of her destiny.

"I'm ready," she said, more confident in herself than she had ever been, at least, she hoped so.

EIGHT

The great double doors creaked in opposition as they opened inwards, revealing a long corridor. Zane and Diana made their way down the hallway of the ancient structure. The doors closed behind them with a significant thud. Diana clasped her hand to her chest, letting out a gasp. She looked back at the door as she continued forward with Zane.

The hallway was lined with great pillars, each one adorned with a torch that lit the way. The fire's light danced merrily across the walls. Creating patterns, like light filtered through water at the bottom of a swimming pool. Diana found the play of light comforting.

Zane led them to the end of the corridor, where it spilled out overlooking a great stadium below. Above them was the open night sky of Sabnare, with its moons overlooking the arena.

Zane began his descent down the stone stairs towards the open field of sand with Diana in tow. Diana looked up and around at all the seating, rising above her, as she continued towards the field. Across the stadium, Diana noticed a doorway under the stands at the far side of the field. She half expected a lion to come charging out for her to battle.

They reached the top of the wall looming over the arena. Zane turned, heading down another set of stairs that led to the ground level behind the field's perimeter wall. They reached the bottom and walked down a narrow passageway next to the stairs they had just taken. An opening was on the side of the wall a few feet away. The opening deposited them onto the field across from the large passageway Diana had spotted before.

Stepping out into the arena, Diana looked up at the moons and stars. She took a turn to look at all the empty rows of seats that stood high above the arena. The walls of the academy reached up, almost swallowing her. Zane stopped once they had almost reached the center of the field.

"Tario!" he called, with his hands up to his mouth.

A rumbling from the tunnel caught Diana's attention. She looked just in time to see a large wave of sand come roaring out of the tunnel, crashing against the side before spilling out into the arena. A tsunami of sand rose before them. The column of sand swelled, towering over them. Diana ducked, covering her head as the wave came crashing down in front of them. Zane's eyes narrowed, and lips puckered as the waves of sand began to encircle them. Diana stood up while shielding her eyes from the raging sand with her arm.

Diana watched Zane, just standing there, unfazed by what was happening around them. Diana's arm lowered, and she started to scan the top of the waves of sand. Her eyes were drawn to a robed figure riding on top of the wall of churning sand. Zane's arms were crossed, and he was strumming his fingers on his arm.

The robed figure continued to speed around them until he stopped in front of them. The sand parted like a curtain behind them and lowered back into the ground until both sides reached the figure, and he was standing on a pillar before them. The column of sand began to lower as steps formed, leading to Zane and Diana. The figure strutted down the stairs, head held high, his chest puffed out.

He sported the traditional stark white sandman hair in a slicked-backed suave ponytail. His immaculately pressed robes were worn very shawl-like, effortlessly flung around his chest and shoulders, revealing a bronzed midriff with a generous length of fabric flowing behind him. Zane cocked his head, slowly blinked, and took a deep breath.

"Seriously, Tario," he said exasperated, "was that really necessary?"

"I wanted to make an entrance for the trainee you were bringing me." Tario looked around, not even acknowledging Diana's presence. "So where is he?"

"Tario, I'd like you to meet Diana," Zane said, "she is your student."

Tario's smile faded from his face. His eyes narrowed, and his nostrils flared as he turned to look at Diana.

"Why would I train a genie?" he said. His disgust was palpable.

"She's not a genie, she's a sandman," Zane replied.

"I don't have time for this," Tario said, gesturing at Diana.

"She is the daughter of Warrick," Zane said sternly, "and she is meant to save Sabnare."

"What exactly is she supposed to save us from?"

Zane paused briefly. Tario looked at him like a matador looks at a bull, challenging him.

"You don't even know what it is that she's supposed to save us from, do you?"

"Warrick told me that it's her destiny to save Sabnare from a great evil, and that is good enough for me!" Zane stared down Tario, daring him to object.

"Why should I care about Warrick's tales?" he asked, "Everyone knows he's a bit off."

Zane sighed and looked at Tario, who stood there, arms crossed. He looked Tario in the eyes.

"Don't do it for Warrick," Zane said, "do it for me."

Tario blushed and turned his head away from Zane's face. His muscles relaxed, and gently, one arm fell to the side as the other still rubbed his bicep. He lifted his head to return Zane's gaze.

"Fine, I'll do it," he turned to Diana, "don't make me regret this."

"I will give you my all," Diana replied, looking directly into Tario's eyes.

"Let's hope that is enough," he said. Tario turned to Zane, "You owe me for this."

"Don't worry, he is very skilled, and you will learn a lot," Zane reassured Diana, "I will be back I need to finish preparations." He looked back at Tario, "Take care of her I'm trusting you. And whatever you do, don't tell Malvin."

Tario began to object before being cut off by Zane, "Promise me."

"Fine," Tario said, his eyes glaring.

Zane looked back at Diana and gave her a rare smile before he disappeared in a swirl of moonlight. Diana looked at where Zane had been standing and wondered what he was taking care of. She wished he could have stayed for her training.

"Let's get started," Tario said, breaking the silence, "do you know anything about your abilities as a sandman?"

"I don't know anything more than what I've seen today. I didn't know I was a sandman or a witch until today."

"Ugh," he replied, "how am I supposed to work with you, it takes years to master all your abilities as a sandman."

"Well, I'm sorry for the inconvenience," she snapped while clenching her fists. "I wish I would have known who and what I really am, but I wasn't given that luxury." Sand began swirling around the base of her feet. "Now I'm doing the best I can with the hand I've been dealt and trying to make the most of it." Her fingers shot out straight as she released her grip and let out a breath. The swirling sand expanded outward and settled. She looked down at her hands as she realized what she had done.

Tario smirked at her. "Okay, I can work with this," he said.

NINE

Tario circled Diana as she stood in the center of the open arena. Assessing her for weakness and planning his attack. The light of the moons of Sabnare did little to dispel the shadows cast by the torches mounted around the arena. Making his movements feel even more intimidating.

"Sandmen have certain abilities to aid them in their work. The first ability is called shifting. Shifting is the ability to control sand." Tario made waved his hand over the ground, and the sand sprung to life. Tiny pillars of sand rose and fell as Tario manipulated them like a marionette. Tario swiftly pulled back his hand and let the sand return lifelessly to the ground. "Your turn," he said, challenging her.

Diana held her hand over the sand, trying to mimic the motions that Tario had made moments before. Her fingers danced in the air. The sand, however, did nothing. Tario watched her failed attempt. Disdain painted across his face.

"You need to feel it, you need to concentrate," he said. "Magic is emotion; you just have to let yourself have it."

Diana focused on the sand, harshly wiggling her fingers like a deranged pianist. The sand began to move, but unlike when Tario had done it before, with each downward stroke of a finger, it made dents in the sand. The sand was sinking into the ground instead of rising upward. Tario rolled his eyes.

"You'll never get it that way," he said, "don't think about what you want to happen, feel it, feel your connection to the sand, let it be an extension of yourself."

Diana tried to calm her mind. She placed her hand over her heart. She focused on the rhythmic beat, letting herself get lost in it. In the still of her mind, another beat began to come into focus. The energy from the sand rose to the surface, beating, complementing her own heart's rhythm.

The energy was all around her; it was the pulse of Sabnare. She opened herself up to the flow of the energy, letting it mix with her own. Creating a magical symphony that was hers alone to hear. Diana's eyes opened, the energy enveloping her. She held her arms at her sides and bent them with her hands palms up. The sand around them began to dance in happy pillars, much like the ones Tario had made before.

"Not bad," Tario said without much sincerity. Diana didn't let it get to her; she was feeling her connection to this place. A snarky comment wasn't going to detract from this first achievement.

"Now let me see what else you can do," Tario said. "Whatever you do, just get used to how your connection to the sand works and feels."

Diana brought her arms around to her front and pushed out. The sand responded. The dancing pillars of sand retreated to join the rest of the sand as it began to form irregular waves. The gentle waves of sand continued to form in front of her and traveled towards the opposite end of the area, where they'd break apart without being able to reach the wall.

"Continue to see if you can intensify the waves," Tario instructed, "see if you can make them larger, faster, and more uniform."

Diana made a pulling-up motion, and the waves began to rise higher than they had before. She then followed through with a push forward, and the waves moved quicker than they had before. She watched as the waves of sand formed at her feet and moved across the ground. She looked behind her and saw that the ground stayed lifelessly inert. Returning her focus to the front, she noticed that the waves were about waist-high on Tario. However, they were parting in front of him and coming back together once it had passed him. Diana realized he was shifting the sand to avoid getting hit by the waves.

She focused, trying to make the wave stay together as it reached Tario's feet. Tario's shifting ability was very solid, and wave after wave continued to part in front of him. She focused, and with a single-handed pushing motion, the wave didn't part before him. The wave passed over his feet, still partially repressed by Tario's shift.

Tario raised an eyebrow, looking up from his feet. He amped up his shift, parting the sand earlier and wider than before.

Diana gave a half smile as her eyes narrowed. She spread her arms and slowly brought her arms together as if to clap but without ever meeting. The sand stirred and changed direction. No longer was Diana the point of origin, but the side walls were. Two sets of sand waves headed for the middle where Tario stood.

Tario causally made a dismissive motion with his hands, making the waves unable to reach him. They crashed into what appeared to be an unseen wall, an immovable fortress that he had formed around him with his shift.

Diana centered herself. Allowing her to feel what she wanted and see it clearly in her mind's eye. The waves of sand grew larger, more powerful, crashing against the barrier. A stormy sea of sand.

Tario's face was smug as he expanded his barrier line. Unbothered. He looked at her, challenging her.

Diana's arms began to quiver. Her hands shaking more violently than the rest of her. She desperately tried to control her focus. Now, her legs shook with fatigue, making it nearly impossible to concentrate. The sand became less uniform and more chaotic as if a hurricane had rolled in.

Diana fell to her knees in the sand as her legs gave way beneath her. As she hit the ground, the sand settled back into its original inert state.

Tario walked over to where she rested in the sand.

"Not bad," he said, "now let's work on the next skill, sand-surfing."

"Okay, just give me a moment."

"Time is not a luxury that you have."

"I know, but I just..."

Tario cut her off. "This is why Zane should be the one in charge of protecting Sabnare. He is already well-trained and has mastered all the skills that a sandman should know. There is nothing you could bring to the table that Zane couldn't."

"But..." she tried again to no avail.

"Zane is one of the most gifted sandmen that Sabnare has ever seen, even if he did study under someone as lax as Warrick. Imagine if he had been trained by a sandman who carried themselves properly like Malvin. It really does speak to his skills that he could overcome the burden of a mentor such as Warrick."

Diana made a sharp movement with her arm, sending a speeding stream of sand directly into the side of Tario's head, momentarily knocking him off balance. A smirk appeared on her face. Diana stood up and dusted herself off.

"Let's continue," she said, locking eyes, a fire burning within her.

Tario stood for a moment and then stepped into a surfing position. He began to glide across the sand, circling her like a shark in the open ocean. Intently watching, looking for any weakness.

"Sand-surfing is a natural progression from the skills you've learned with basic sand-shifting," he said while continuing to circle her. "Like before, you want to move the sand, but you move along with it." He glared down at her. "You need to control the consistency of the sand beneath you so that it moves you." Tario came to a stop directly in front of her, their noses almost touching. "What are you waiting for," he said in a huff, "start trying."

Diana focused, feeling the energy flowing up around her feet. She pushed off with one leg like a figure skater. Promptly falling to the ground.

Returning to her feet, she tried again. This time, she managed to glide a few feet before coming to a stop. Diana was reminded of the feeling during the volleyball game. Focusing on that feeling, she pushed off again. In her mind's eye, she saw herself as an Olympic skater moving effortlessly across the rink. This time, Diana went farther.

"Keep going, don't stop!" Tario shouted.

Diana pushed off and, this time continued the skating motion. Side to side. Swish, swish. She put her arms slightly out with her palms back, willing the sand to move her.

She picked up a little speed. Working her way around the arena, she stumbled a little but managed to keep her balance. She looked over at Tario as he watched her.

"You're going to use up too much energy that way and tire yourself out," he snapped, "try to move less."

Diana knew he was right, but it didn't make his tone any less condescending. *Dick.* She brought her feet together, trying to be still while still riding the sand. The sand beneath her shifted at a faster pace, and she promptly fell to the ground. Before Tario could say anything, she got back up. Diana stepped into a stance where one foot was forward, and another was behind her. She envisioned that there was solid, dense sand beneath her. She focused on her shift, moving forward. She was still slightly wobbly, but progress was being made.

"Better," Tario sneered, "but let's take it to the next level."

"What's the next level?"

Tario sand-surfed his way over to her with an almost playful grin on his face. He reached out and tapped Diana right on the tip of her nose.

"Tag, you're it," he said.

Tario rose up on a wave of sand, speeding away from Diana. He turned around, still standing high above her. He brought his wave of sand to a stationary position, locking eyes with Diana. He motioned with his hands to come after him.

Diana pushed off in Tario's direction. She dug into her stance. Her forward arm bent at the elbow, the other trailing behind her. She launched in Tario's direction, struggling to keep her balance.

He stood his ground. Just before Diana could reach him, life returned to Tario's wave, moving out of her way.

Diana stumbled as she turned to follow. Crashing and rolling across the sand. Without missing a beat, she got up, crouched low to the ground, and continued the pursuit of Tario.

Diana's control was improving as she chased Tario. She zigged and zagged as she followed him. She reached out to tag Tario.

Just as she tried to tag him, Tario turned on a dime. Diana kept going, slamming into a wall. As much as she hated it, she had to admit his reflexes were impressive. Diana shook her head. She didn't have time to contemplate his skills. She adjusted her robes and raced towards Tario.

Diana sped up as she tried to catch up with Tario and get in front of his path. She closed the distance. Diana executed a sideways turn, cutting off Tario. Before she could reach out and tag him, Tario launched himself off his sand wave and flipped over Diana, landing on a new wave that rose to meet him. Diana watched in shock for just a moment before coming back to reality and continuing her pursuit.

Tario turned at the far part of the arena and began his way down the center of the field. Diana trailed close behind him. She was gaining on him quickly when she had an idea.

She focused on the energy of the sand and how it mixed with hers. With an upward gathering motion from her arms, two walls of sand shot up, creating a barrier in front of Tario.

Tario faltered, and the walls knocked him off of his wave. Just as he landed on the ground, Diana zipped by and tagged him. She turned into a stop and reached out a hand to Tario. Scowling, he looked at her hand and then up at her smiling face. He reached out, and Diana helped him up to his feet.

"What's next, teach?" Diana asked with a sly smile, wiping a strand of hair out of her face. Tario raised an eyebrow and cracked a smile that disappeared as fast as it arrived.

"That wasn't awful," he said, brushing himself off and regaining his composure. "The next skill is crucial but should be easier than what we've already covered."

"What is it?"

"Moon-beaming," he said, "it a type of travel where you start in one place. . ."

Tario was suddenly surrounded by swirling moonlight and, with a flash, disappeared. Then, across the arena, the lights reappeared and revealed Tario as they dissipated.

"To another."

Diana remembered how Phelipe had left in a swirl of lights and how beautiful it was. She was eager to learn how to do this herself. This skill was something that could come in very handy.

"How does it work?" she asked.

"All you have to do is think about where you want to be and let the moon's energy course through you and take you where you want to be."

"Okay, that sounds fairly straight to the point. Pick a place and let the moon take you there."

Diana closed her eyes, picturing the other side of the arena where Tario was standing. She held her head up so that her face could bask in the light of the moons. A warmth washed down her body as she bathed in the energy of the moons. The cozy energy flowed around her. The hairs on Diana's arms stood up and began to tingle. She opened her eyes as tiny orbs of moonlight danced all around her. Dancing until the orbs flashed, and all she could see was light.

Diana's body lifts from the ground, her toes just above the sand. As the light began to break, she could see her surroundings come back into focus through the dancing light. As the light retreated,

Diana came crashing out of the sky. Landing directly on top of Tario, sending them both to the ground in a heap.

"Get off of me, "Tario yelled, shoving Diana off of him.

"I'm so sorry," she stammered, scrambling to her feet. She tried to lend a hand to Tario to help him up. He swatted her away and got back up himself.

"Your aim is shit," he growled, "try again, away from me this time."

Diana decided it was best to just continue and to do what he said. Again, she focused on where she wanted to be. She picked the center of the arena. She envisioned herself swept away by the moonlight to that spot. The light swirled around her, and when it finished, she saw she was centerfield. However, she was slightly off the ground. She dropped to one knee, bracing her fall as she finished moon-beaming.

Diana dusted herself off as she stood up. She really needed to work on her landings. Before Tario could try to yell at her, she was at it again. Diana bathed herself in the light of the moons. This time, when she reappeared, she was on the far side of the arena, staring back at Tario. She had stuck the landing after moon-beaming. Knowing that there was no time to rest or congratulate herself, Diana moon-beamed again. Appearing right next to where Tario was standing.

She was catching on to moon-beaming faster than she did to shifting. She looked at Tario, awaiting further instructions. Tario looked at her and then turned, looking up at the rows of stadium seating that rose above them. Without breaking his gaze, he gave his next instruction.

"I want you to moon-beam yourself up into the stands and then back here."

Diana followed his gaze and began to focus on that area of the stands. The light whizzed around her until it hit its brightest intensity, and she vanished. When the light faded from her eyes, she was right where she had planned on appearing. Another swirl of light appeared as she beamed back to where Tario waited for her. Tario gave a less than enthusiastic shrug while pursing out his lips and raising his eyebrow.

"Next lesson," he said, "invisibility."

Diana's eyebrows raised. Invisibility also sounded rather useful.

"Now invisibility works by reflecting moonlight around you so that the mundane people can't see you. It is much less effective on magical people. Its main function is so that sandman can move about the bedrooms of people undetected to deliver dream sand."

Tario surrounded himself in moonlight. It was as if a translucent syrup had been spilled over his head. Light quickly covered his body, and the light defused around him. Diana stared at where Tario stood. The air there appeared to be a bit blurry. She walked around, and as she did, she could see light glints of light and contours of shadow. The shimmery light parted down the center as Tario revealed himself.

"Being invisible is less effective during the day, and depending on what other light sources are around those can as limit how invisible you appear. It works much like moon-beaming, but instead of feeling the moon's energy whisk you away, you focus on it, engulfing and reflecting around you. Almost as if it's a second skin."

"Alright, let me give this a go," she said.

Diana summoned the light of the moon around her. She pictured it wrapping around her like a large blanket, protecting her from the cold. She felt the warmth of the light spreading all across her body. She looked down at her arms. She could see them, but she couldn't see them at the same time. There was a faint outline, but the light was doing its job and rendering her practically transparent.

"How's this?" This she asked Tario.

"Not bad," he paused. "For a beginner."

Diana knew that was about as high of praise as she was going to get from Tario. She let the light that blanketed her lift away. Once again, she was fully visible in the arena. Diana removed strands of hair from her face and wiped away some sweat.

"What's next?" Diana asked, breathing heavily.

"The last thing I have for you is the basics of dream sand. Dream sand is what we use to help people fall asleep, and it is the vehicle in which we deliver dreams. Sandmen who are chosen to deliver dreams receive satchels of dream sand from the castle in the center of the Desert of Dreams. A large diamond rests above the castle, producing the dream sand."

"Hold on one second. I want to see something."

Diana pulled out the scroll her father had made for her. Its wings flapped as it sprung to life and hovered at face level. She pulled up a picture of the Diamond of Dreams. It was stunning. The diamond appeared to be made of the same amethyst as the mountains that encompassed Sabnare. Tario continued to explain without taking his eyes off the scroll.

"Dream sand is very potent; it takes very little to do the job. Just a light sprinkle, and you can put someone to sleep. Just aim for the eyes. If they are already asleep, it will help their sleep be sounder and awaken their ability to dream."

As Tario spoke, the scroll showed images of pouches filled with purple dream sand. It then brought up diagrams on how to properly deliver the sand.

"Dream sand doesn't work on sandmen," Tario continued. "It is meant for humans; however, it also works on animals. This keeps you safe if you're ever in a house that is guarded by a dog or any other animal that could alert others to your presence. Magical creatures are usually not as receptive to dream sand. Especially creatures from Sabnare like the slumbra."

The scroll brought up pictures of a fearsome-looking creature. It was the largest snake Diana had ever seen. It was crested like a cobra, with spikes running down each side and glowing patterns that almost looked like a paisley print. Its dark purple glowing eyes showed no emotion. Its long, glistening fangs appeared to be almost as long as she was tall. *At least it's not bees.* She shuddered at the thought.

"Legend has it that slumbra's venom was a key ingredient that witches would use in sleeping potions and curses. It is believed that just one drop of its venom was enough to put someone to sleep for a thousand years, but it's hard to say for sure. The only person I know of who has faced a slumbra and survived is Zane."

Tario beamed with pride. He was completely lost in thought until he noticed Diana watching him. His facial expressions quickly hardened. He looked back at the image of the slumbra present on Diana's scroll.

"If you ever see one," he turned to look at her, "just run."

Diana collapsed, breathing heavily, into one of the seats at the top of the arena that overlooked the field. She dabbed sweat from her brow with the sleeve of her robes as Tario settled into the seat beside her. She had been training with Tario for hours. Working the techniques over and over, including combinations of the techniques.

"I don't think there is anything more for me to show you in the time we have," Tario said. "I have given you all the basics faster than I've ever had to before. You did well, considering the circumstances."

Diana looked at Tario with his gruff exterior and smiled. He was almost being complementary. She was very proud of herself and the progress she made. It was the hardest thing she had ever done, and she did it relatively successfully.

"So that's everything?" She asked.

"Well, no," he said, "there is usually more I cover during basic training. I usually like to go over the lost sandman powers."

"What are those?"

"There were certain abilities that sandmen used to learn; some were banned, such as dream diving. Others were forgotten over time.

Legend has it that there are words of power that a select few sandmen had control over. Those sandmen were able to manipulate items that held those words in their names. They called those special sandmen sandmages."

Diana listened, shifting in her seat. Every one of her muscles ached. She had never been so drained in all her life. However, sitting at the top of the stadium and letting the moons shine down on her seemed to be helping her recharge.

She was starting to get comfortable, the fresh night air filling her lungs. A crisp breeze blew in from the ocean, helping her cool down.

Diana's moment of serenity came to an end, with a strange sound from outside breaking the silence. Tario shot to his feet to look over the side of the wall.

"What was that?" Diana asked, standing up to look over the edge.

"I have no idea," Tario replied.

Tario grabbed Diana's hand. Without a word, they were surrounded by a flurry of light. Her eyes focused as the light subsided. They were now standing outside by the edge of the pond that she had passed earlier. Near the edge of the pond, there was a sandman lying in a heap of robes. She rushed over with Tario right behind her. Tario knelt down, turning the robed figure over. Diana let out a gasp. She couldn't believe her eyes.

"Phelipe!" she screamed, "what happened, are you alright?

Phelipe coughed and reached out for Diana. She dropped down beside him and took his hand; it was cold and clammy. His chest rose and fell with each labored breath. Diana looked him over, trying to see what was wrong. The color in his face had become faded and ashy. His sparkling eyes were dull imitations of what they once were.

"It was a trap," he wheezed.

Tears welled up in Diana's eyes. She looked up at Tario.

"Go find Zane," she said, her eyes pleading.

Tario looked at them, frozen. His mouth was agape, and eyes wide with shock.

"Now!" Diana yelled.

Tario shook his head, snapping out of it. With a swirl of light, he moon-beamed away in search of Zane.

Diana helped to make Phelipe comfortable, resting his head on her knees. He gave a slight smile before having another coughing fit.

"Shhh," she said, stroking his hair, "Zane will be here soon, and he'll know what to do."

"You have to stop her," he said weakly.

"Stop who?"

"The soothsayer," he said, coughing. A confused look washed over Diana's face. Before she could ask a question, Phelipe began to struggle, trying to reach into his robes.

"I managed to grab this on my way out." He handed Diana an ornate glass bottle encrusted with purple shards.

"What is it?"

"It's an empty genie bottle."

Diana looked at the bottle in her hands. She ran her fingers over the bottle and its chunky amethyst topper.

"What am I supposed to do with this?" she asked.

"Whatever you want," he gasped, "I just didn't want her to have it. Keep it safe."

Diana stored the bottle away in her robes. She looked around frantically, searching for signs of Zane and Tario.

"Who or what is this soothsayer, what does she want?"

"I don't know."

Swirling moonlight caught Diana's eye. It faded away to reveal Zane and Tario.

"Zane," she cried out. "Thank god you're here, please do something."

Zane walked over and knelt by Phelipe's side. Zane's normally emotionless face contorted into worry. He looked over his friend and took his hand.

"What happened here?" Zane asked.

"He said that it was the soothsayer, and it was a trap."

"A soothsayer, here?" Zane's eyes widened, and his lips pursed. His eyes flitted around from person to person. Phelipe let out a series of brutal coughs.

"I don't have much time," Phelipe said.

"Zane, isn't there something you can do?" Diana pleaded.

"I've never seen anything like this," he said, "I don't know what I can do."

Diana had tears pouring down her face. She squeezed Phelipe's hand tighter, holding it to her chest.

"I'm so happy I got to meet you, Diana," he said, "the first female sandman."

Tario scoffed. Diana wiped away her tears. She looked into his kind eyes. They seemed even dimmer than before. Phelipe let out another series of coughs as Diana held him tight. He looked up at Diana.

"Meet your destiny, Diana," he whispered, "you are Sabnare's greatest hope."

Phelipe let out a gasp. The last of the light faded from his eyes. His body lay limp in Diana's arm. Tears freely poured from her eyes as she stared down at Phelipe's lifeless body.

A gust of wind flowed over her. Phelipe's body shifted in her lap and slowly began to dissolve into sand, moving slowly up from his feet, dancing away in the wind. Finally, his face was the last of him fade away and rejoin the sands of Sabnare. All that was left was a set of robes and a memory.

Diana wailed as she held onto the last grains of Phelipe. A pain ripped through her heart like nothing she had ever felt before. Zane walked over behind Diana. He crouched down and placed his hands on her arms. He gently guided her to her feet while her fists shook uncontrollably.

A sound in the distance caught the attention of Zane and Tario. A group of sandmen were headed their way.

"They must have heard the commotion," Tario said.

"We have to go," Zane said to an inconsolable Diana.

Tario walked over to the group.

"We have to go right now," Tario said, "unless you're ready to explain all this."

Zane looked at the crowd in the distance. Keeping one hand on Diana, he reached out and placed a hand on Tario. Tario tensed at the touch. Light surrounded the group. In a flash, Zane moon-beamed the group away, leaving nothing but a few gusts of swirling sand and a set of robes where they once stood.

CHAPTER

ELEVEN

Stacks of scrolls and journals were spread out over the floor, surrounding Yume where she sat reading. She continued paging through a journal when a commotion from outside made her tear herself away and look towards the door.

The door opened into curtains, and in walked Tario, Diana, and Zane. Zane locked the door without missing a beat. Yume stood there, stunned at the flurry of activity that just came crashing in on her. Diana crumpled to the floor, her fists shaking in front of her.

"What happened," Yume said, hovering over to Diana. Yume placed her trunk on her knee.

"There was an incident," Zane said, "a sandman was killed."

"Are you serious?"

"He said it was a trap and that there was a soothsayer," Tario added.

"Where was he when this happened?" Yume asked.

"He had been summoned to the castle to start work," Zane explained, "we ran into him on our way to Diana's training."

"Who was it?"

"Phelipe," he answered.

Yume floated backward, covering her mouth with her paw. She could barely process what she was hearing: death and soothsayers. Yume glanced at the pile of journals.

"Wait a minute, did you say soothsayer?" Yume asked.

"Did I stutter? "Tario sneered.

"Tario!" Zane scolded.

Tario sank into himself and took a few steps back from the group. His gaze moved down to the floor, no longer making eye contact with the group. Yume, ignoring Tario's comment, floated to the stack of journals. She feverishly tossed several aside with her trunk and flipped it open. She scanned the page with the tip of her trunk.

"Here it is!" she said, bringing the journal over to Zane, "I thought that sounded familiar."

Zane looked down at the journal before him. It was Warrick's handwriting. There was a small passage that read:

> I have tried to warn them about the soothsayer and the visions. No one is taking the threat seriously. I fear I will have to take things into my own hands for the good of Sabnare. There are very few that I can trust with this information. I will have to set pieces in motion to prevent a disaster.

Zane was stunned at what he had just read. This journal was centuries old, how long could Warrick have been preparing?

"Why didn't he tell me about this?" Zane asked.

Tario reached out and grabbed the journal. He scanned the entry and chuckled to himself.

"I guess this explains why he would always disappear for periods of time."

"He could have taken me with him," Zane said, "I could have helped him!"

Diana stood up, regaining some composure.

"Yume, would you grab a cup from the kitchen for me?" she asked.

Yume returned with a clear glass. Diana's heart felt heavy as she carefully emptied the sandy remnants of Phelipe into the cup. She gently placed it down on the desk and walked over to Tario. She took the journal from him and read the passage. Every bit of new information seemed to come with even more questions. Diana had trouble keeping it all together.

"So, what's a soothsayer, and what do we do now?" Diana asked.

Zane stood in contemplation.

"Well, a soothsayer is a witch with the ability to see the future. After all that's happened, I think that we need to head to the castle. There may be further clues to what we are facing," Zane said.

"So do we just moon-beam to the castle?" Diana asked.

"The castle is protected from moon-beaming," Zane explained, "there are only a few places in the castle used to receive moon-beaming. We are going to need to be more inconspicuous with our arrival."

"How do you propose getting to the castle then?" Tario asked.

"We will have to cross the Desert of Dreams," Zane replied, "and it won't be easy there are many dangers that can be found in the desert."

"There is very little water in the Desert of Dreams, and there are fearsome creatures like the slumbra to contend with," Yume added.

"I think what makes the most sense is to go in on a sorina with the supply shipment to the castle," Zane thought out loud, "I believe there's one scheduled to leave tomorrow morning."

"How are you going to keep her hidden with all those people that deliver the shipment?" Tario asked.

Zane cocked his head in thought. Yume was pacing in midair. Tario walked over and sank into the couch, waiting for an answer.

"I guess," Zane said, "the time has come to introduce Diana to the rest of Sabnare."

"Are you really prepared to do that? "Asked Tario.

"I don't see another option."

"Everyone has a right to know what's going on," Yume added.

"Tario, I need you to go gather everyone in the center of the village," Zane said, "Yume, Diana, and myself will gather the supplies we need, and then we will meet you there shortly."

Zane let Tario out of the front door while Yume and Diana packed whatever they thought would come in handy. Zane hoped this would work. He didn't see there being any other choice. Soon, Sabnare would know about the danger they were facing. He looked at Yume and Diana. Hopefully, together, they would have what it takes.

~

The crowd of sandmen waited anxiously beneath the flowing drapery that hung over the town square to find out why they had been summoned. Whispered rumors flew about. They looked to where a makeshift platform had been shifted out of sand. Tario waited off to the side of the platform next to a small alleyway between two buildings. Two clusters of swirling light appeared, followed by a swirl of smoke. The lights and smoke cleared to reveal Zane, Diana, and Yume.

"Everyone is here, waiting to hear your announcement," Tario said.

Zane stood with his solemn face, closed his eyes, and took in a deep breath.

"Here we go," he said, He turned to Diana, "keep your robes up and face covered until I introduce you."

"Sure," she said. Diana adjusted her robes, keeping her face hidden as best she could.

Zane gave her a nod of approval. He looked at Tario and motioned for him to lead the way. The group exited the alley and waited by the side of the platform as Tario climbed the steps. He reached the center and turned to the murmuring crowd. Tario cleared his throat forcefully. A hush fell over the crowd as they waited to hear what Tario had to say.

"I'm sure you are all wondering why I called you all here," he said, "so I give you the man who asked that I bring you together." Zane stepped forward onto the platform.

"Thank you, Tario, for bringing us all together," he said, as Tario walked back to where Zane had been standing next to Diana and Yume, "My friends, I won't prolong this. Sabnare is in great danger."

The crowd burst into nervous chatter, looking at one another. Zane continued over the murmurs.

"Warrick tried to prepare for this, but no one believed this day would come. Sandmen have been going missing. Now Warrick is also missing, and Phelipe..." he paused, "is dead."

The crowd started shouting in disbelief. Panic was taking hold.

"Please try to remain calm. We don't know a lot at the moment but here's what do know. Warrick has been preparing for this on his own for centuries because no one would listen to him. He told me about a great threat that would be coming, but he never went into detail on what that danger was. We now know, thanks to Phelipe, that a soothsayer has taken over the castle at the center of the Desert of Dreams. Warrick left a few weeks ago when sandmen started disappearing. He feared that the great danger was finally upon us. Warrick left me with instructions; he told me that if he didn't return, that I was to seek out the one and only person he believed could protect Sabnare. I would like to introduce that person to you now."

Zane motioned for Diana. Tario and Yume lead her up the platform. All the sandmen's eyes locked on Diana as she walked. Her ears were filled with their jumbled muttering. She reached the center, standing next to Zane. She looked up at him. Zane nodded at her. Diana turned to the crowd. She lifted her head and pulled back her hood. Her ponytail fell free, swinging in the breeze.

The crowd gasped, then erupted into a mix of confusion and rage.

"Is this some kind of joke?" shouted an older balding sandman.

"A genie is our savior!" scoffed another.

The crowd became louder and louder. Diana's breathing grew increasingly rapid as she no longer was able to make out individual voices. Her eyes darted from face to face, trying to find a place to focus.

Zane tried to calm the crowd so that he could continue. The sandmen continued to shout over one another, unable to hear Zane.

Yume stepped forward and let out a mighty blast of sound from her trunk. The crowd fell silent. Stunned by the sound of Yume's roaring trumpet.

"Thank you, Yume," Zane said, "Everyone, this is Diana. Daughter of Warrick."

The crowd all began talking at once. Zane held up a hand until they calmed down.

"I know this comes as a shock for most of you," he said, "but she is a sandman and a witch, and she is here for all of us."

The disapproval from the crowd washed over Diana like a high tide, threatening to drown her as she fought to stay afloat. Everyone's eyes glared at her with burning judgment. She scanned the group that stood before her, avoiding eye contact. Zane's words rattled incoherently in the echo chamber of her mind. People whispered and pointed, with scowls etched across their faces. A voice shouted out above the crowd.

"She's not even a real sandman," said a young sandman with wavy shoulder-length hair. "How are we supposed to trust her?"

Diana looked out and met his eyes. He was shaking with a mix of fear and anger. She wasn't sure how she could reach these people, but she knew she had to try.

"I understand that many of you are skeptical of me," she shouted, "and you know what?" She paused, "so am I."

The crowd began to talk again. Their faces were painted with confusion and apprehension. Diana continued.

"When Zane showed up, I could barely believe what was happening. I had no idea that I was a witch or a sandman. These parts of myself had been hidden away from me so that I could one day stand here and fight to protect a land I had never heard of, for people I had never known, and a father I had never met. I've never truly excelled at anything in my life, which I guess one can expect when you are so utterly disconnected from who you are. Unable to be your authentic self. But I had a choice. I could stay and continue living my life as it had always been, or I could stop everything and give my all just on the off chance that I actually could help. Even if I wasn't sure, I fully believed it. I thought that if there was even a slight chance that I could help, it was worth it. I may not have the same experience as all of you. I may have just learned about who I am and my powers. But since I arrived, I have worked hard to get a handle on my powers and learn all I can in a very short time. And I will continue to work hard and do all I can to protect Sabnare. That is the choice I've made!"

Diana looked out at all the sandmen. As she watched, many of their faces softened. Some remained unmoved. All she could hope for was an ounce of empathy, she spoke from her heart, hoping that would be enough.

"Friends, I fear that Diana's arrival could be found out before we can make a move," Zane said. "But we want to try and keep the element of surprise. Please keep this here, between us. If you have correspondence with anyone at the castle, do not mention what has been discussed here. Our hope is to sneak into the castle on a sorina with the next shipment of supplies. I hope that you will allow us to do this so we can fight for Sabnare."

The crowd seemed more receptive after hearing from Zane. The murmur was less angry yet still apprehensive. Worry was still apparent on their faces. Diana could hardly blame them. They just found out that their world is in danger, a friend is dead, and some unknown girl is supposed to save them all. She wasn't the only one with a lot to take in.

"I will grant you passage on the sorina," said one of the sandmen. Diana looked to see who said it. All the others had turned to look at him. He was about a foot shorter than Zane, and his white buzz cut popped against his ebony skin. He was the most muscular sandman that Diana had seen since arriving in Sabnare.

"Thank you, Raza," Zane said, "let's make arrangements. Everyone else, thank you for coming, and please keep Diana's presence here a secret."

The crowd began to disperse. There were flashes of light as some people moon-beamed and flurries of sand as others sand-surfed away. Zane walked down to Raza to make plans, with Yume following close behind. Tario hung back against the wall.

After finishing with Raza, Zane and Yume headed back to Diana. Tario walked over to the group.

"We are all set to ride on the sorina," Zane said.

"When do we leave?" Tario asked.

"Tario, I'm going to ask you to stay here," Zane said. "We are going to need someone here to watch over the village and let us know if something happens."

"I can be much more useful going with you."

"I need you to take care of things here."

"Fine," Tario huffed, crossing his arms.

"Thank you, Tario," Zane said, "Diana, you, Yume, and I will leave in a few hours. So, you should get some rest."

The group headed back towards Warrick's to grab the last few things they needed and to get some rest. Tario headed back to his place to rest before seeing the others off. Diana grew tired as the day started to catch up with her. She stretched her arms above her head and let out a yawn. Her eyes grew heavy as they reached Warrick's house.

Diana curled up in the soft, warm bed, shutting her eyes. Yume curled up at her feet while Zane took the couch. Diana drifted off to sleep, the events of the day replaying in her head and thinking about what was yet to come.

TWELVE

The sand crunched beneath their feet as Zane led Diana and Yume toward the rendezvous point. The sorina was being loaded behind the academy. As they rounded the pond, Diana hung back for a moment. Zane and Yume noticed that they had gotten ahead of Diana. They stopped, turning to look at her.

Diana pulled out a vial that held the remains of Phelipe. She held it close to her heart for a moment. She could almost see his face reflected across the water. Diana felt a tap on her shoulder. She turned to see Yume floating beside her.

"Diana," she said softly, "it's time to go."

Diana looked out one last time over the water and tucked away the vial in her pouch. She turned, reaching out her hand, and Yume took it in her trunk as they headed toward Zane, who had continued on.

Zane turned the corner behind the academy. Diana and Yume picked up their pace, trying to catch up. Diana rounded the corner, coming to an abrupt stop. Her heart pounded, and she froze in place.

Towering over her was a large bird. Startled, the creature let out an ear-splitting screech. The bird turned and ran on its large legs. It was the size of an ostrich but had the body and flowing plumage of a peacock. Its head had a ferocious curved beak, like that of an eagle. It was actually quite a beautiful animal, now that Diana had a chance to process it.

"What was that," she asked Yume.

"That's an ostrock; sandmen use them to ride on and to help protect shipments to the castle."

The ostrock had wandered over to a group of sandmen huddled near a large vessel. It looked like some kind of combination ship and sled. The deck of the ship was adorned with what looked like a Japanese temple, complete with red torii gates. The beauty of the ornate craft looked like it belonged in a museum. Diana saw Zane standing with the group and made her way over with Yume. Diana's mouth hung open as she neared the great ship. Zane noticed her expression.

"That is a sorina," he said. "This is how we will travel across the Desert of Dreams."

Diana watched as the sandmen worked like a fine-tuned machine. They would use their shift to move crates around the back and into the cargo bay. Smaller boxes were shifted upwards on pillars of sand to the upper deck, where other sandmen shifted them onto the deck safely.

At the front of the sorina, other sandmen were harnessing up a flock of ostrock. Three rows of ostrock were hitched to the front of the sorina. The ostrock were beautiful, most of which were blueish green in color. Others were pinks and purples; they were the most stunning of jewel tones, while a select few were vibrant white.

A mounted white ostrock strode over to where they were standing. Diana recognized the rider as Raza.

"We are almost finished loading the sorina," Raza said, "we will be leaving shortly." He looked directly at Diana. "It is my great pleasure to help you on your journey." He nodded his head and then took off on his ostrock.

"Let's get to our cabin," Zane said.

Zane rose up on a mound of sand, hopping onto the upper deck. Yume followed behind with an effortless leap, smoke trailing from around her feet, and landed on the deck. Diana focused her shift and began to rise, not nearly as quickly or gracefully as Zane had. She leapt over to the sorina. As she landed, she lost her footing. Diana went tumbling into Zane, who caught her.

"Thank you," she said.

Zane nodded, "this way." He started walking down the deck towards the cabin. As they passed, Diana noticed the other sandmen staring at her out of the corners of their eyes. None of them dared to make direct eye contact with her.

Zane turned a corner, stepping down into a covered section of the sorina. Yume hovered behind, followed by Diana.

Diana was now walking down a large hallway lined by doors. About halfway down, Zane stopped at a door.

"This is it," he said.

He opened the door, letting Diana and Yume enter before him. The room was immaculately furnished. A large bench circled the room. It was plush with throw pillows all about. Three lengths of fabric hung down from the center of the ceiling and then down the walls.

Diana and Zane set down the pouches they had filled. They had grabbed only what they thought would be essential. Luckily, Diana found a spell that made containers hold more than they appeared to in the spell book from her mom. After several tries to execute the spell, it made their pouches hold nearly endless amounts of items.

The sound of bells filled the cabins of the sorina. Diana looked to Zane.

"That means we are about to head out, it's the last call for all to get on board," he said, answering her silent question.

"Let's go out to the front and watch," Yume said.

"I'd love that," Diana said.

Zane flashed a rare smile, "Sure, let's go."

The group gathered on the deck near the front of the sorina.

Diana leaned forward with her hands on the rail. She could see the rows of harnessed ostrock, with other mounted ostrock on the sides of the sorina. Diana watched as Raza rode his white ostrock out in front of the flock.

Raza's ostrock let out a screech. The others answered its call in a magical symphony. The white ostrock lifted and fanned out its tail feathers while they started glowing with an aura around them. The other ostrock followed the alpha's lead. They splayed out their many-colored tail feathers, making them glow with their aura. The flock let out a harmonized song.

Diana held tight to the railing as the sorina shifted under her feet as if it was lifting off of the ground.

"What's happening?" Diana asked, reaffirming her grip on the rail in front of her.

"Ostrock can summon a barrier with their tail feathers," he said, "they spread it around the sides and under the sorina helping it glide across the sand as they pull it. Some sandmen take turns shifting sand to help propel the sorina so the ostrock don't overwork themselves."

Raza's ostrock threw back its head and let out three squawks that came to a crescendo before starting to march forward. The flock answered the call and started to pull forward as sandmen in the back shifted sand to help the sorina shove off. The sorina lurched forward and began to glide across the sand.

It rounded the side of the academy, heading towards the village. Diana saw Tario standing, arms crossed, leaning against the wall of the academy. Upon seeing the sorina, Tario turned, walking back into the academy.

Diana looked forward as they began to pick up speed. She could now see the village visible in the distance. The traveling party followed a path that ran beside the village, leading to an opening in the mountains.

The ostrock charged forward into the cavern. They followed the twists and turns of the mountain path. The sorina rounded a final curve, and the cavern opened up to reveal a sprawling desert. The Desert of Dreams. Diana could see the glowing mountain range that bordered the desert. Looking up, she could see all the moons of Sabnare ranging in size and color. The slightly purple-hued sand of the desert sparked under the light of the moon and glowing mountains. It was the first time since she had arrived that she could just take in how beautiful Sabnare was.

"We have several hours until we hit our first stop," Zane said, "we should head back to our room and continue going through the scrolls and journals."

"You should also read more of that spell book from your mother," Yume added.

"You're right, I need to be prepared for anything that could happen," Diana said.

The group returned to the room and got to work. Yume spread out scrolls and journals on the floor. She handed a scroll to Zane and took a scroll for herself. Diana took out the book of spells her mother had put together. They all made themselves at home on the benches and got to work. Diana flipped through the spells that were bookmarked first, wanting to see what her mother thought would be important and useful. There were spells for healing, protection, binding, and much more. She flipped to the front of the book. There was a note written on the first page from her mom.

My little witch,

May this book guide you and inspire you. Your journey as a witch won't always be easy. Especially with your special circumstances, but may you follow your heart and your witch's intuition. All magical beings have abilities. Every race has spells they can cast, usually limited to their particular field of magic, to enhance the gifts they already have. Witches are magic. We can create spells for almost any purpose. All witches have an ability they can use without the aid of spells, what that is and when it will appear depends on the witch. There are many gifts, such as being able to move objects with your mind, there are witches who can control the four elements, and even a rare few who can create anything they can see in their mind. What your ability will be is unknown, and with you being half sandman, I'm not sure if that will affect it. Please keep yourself safe, and trust the words in this book and the items you were given. You will do great things.

Love, Mom.

Diana set down the book. She had barely thought of the items she had been given. She had her wand stored in a special pocket of her robes, along with the key from her father. Her bag of sand was attached to her hip, which covered the dream catcher. She held the dream catcher in front of her. It was beautiful with its purple beads and what she now knew were ostrock feathers dangling from the bottom. Yume looked up and saw her examining the dream catcher.

"Dream catchers protect you from bad dreams," Yume said, "They shield you from the pain of nightmares. It only lets the good dreams through. Of course, when you don't have a dream catcher, baku are always around to devour your bad dreams."

"So, it's like a dream shield, huh?"

As Diana spoke the words, the dream catcher began to glow and spin in the air. It grew in size as it spun, floating over to her left. Diana lifted her arm in a move of protection. The dream catcher stopped spinning, attaching itself to her arm as straps formed. The glowing faded, revealing an ornate shield of purple crystal. The design of the dream catcher remained etched across the side, and the ostrock feathers had wrapped their way up the sides and crystallized as well. Zane dropped the scroll he was reading and stood up, mouth open.

"Did you cast a spell to do that?" he asked.

"No, I'm not sure how I did it."

"You don't think . . ." Yume trailed off, looking at Zane.

"I do, it's one of the lost sandman powers," he said, "the ability to control words related to dreaming and the objects attached to them. When she thought about the dream catcher as a shield, that's exactly what it became."

Diana stood up and lifted her arm. The shield was surprisingly light. She spun around, trying to get a feel for it.

"Do you think maybe it's because she's half witch?" Yume asked.

"It very well could be; she has all the powers of a sandman and a witch, and those powers are going to mingle and enhance each other," Zane said. "It makes sense that her witch magic could amplify parts of sandman magic. They called those who could use these abilities sandmages, which seems more than fitting in this case. Diana, can you try returning it to its original form?"

Diana looked down at the shield, remembering the dream catcher it had once been. The shield began to shake and lightly glow, then stopped. She looked puzzled and tried again, achieving the same result.

"The power is in the words," Zane said, "I think it has to be spoken to activate the magic."

"Dream catcher," she said. The shield began to glow, spinning as it detached from her arm. It shrunk down in size, and the feathers came loose, dangling at the bottom as it stopped spinning. The dream catcher floated down and reattached itself to her robes.

"That is amazing!" Yume cheered.

"I'm glad I thought to give some attention to the items my parents gave me."

"That's good thinking. I'm sure each item was given for a good reason," Zane said.

"Have either of you found anything more about this soothsayer or where my father has gone?"

"I haven't found anything of significance," Yume said.

"I'm trying to piece together entries by dates, remembering what Warrick had me doing at those times," Zane said, "hopefully some of the pieces connect."

Yume suddenly stood at attention. Her ears twitched, and she began smelling the air. Her eyes grew wide when she locked on a scent.

"Yume, what's wrong?" Diana asked.

Before Yume could answer, bells started ringing, and the sorina came to a halt. Zane fell onto the bench and Diana to the floor. Yume vanished in a puff of smoke.

"Where did she go?" Diana asked.

"Let's follow her," Zane said, taking Diana by the hand.

Her vision burled as they were surrounded by swirling light. When Diana could see again, they were standing at the front of the sorina. Yume was standing there, with her front legs on the railing, looking over the wall.

Zane and Diana approached her. When they looked over the side, they could see an enormous herd of baku surrounding the sorina. There were all shapes, sizes and colors. Some looked like tapirs similar to Yume; others were larger and more ferocious looking. Some had bodies like tigers and leopards, while their heads resembled elephants with smokey manes. Many had large tusks.

The baku bellowed from their trunks. Some were at a standoff with the ostrock, who displayed their tail plumage and extended the crests on their heads.

Baku circled the sorina by air, smoke billowing from their wrists and ankles as they took to the sky. Two baku stepped forward from the herd. The harnessed ostrock backed up and huddled together, facing out the best they could. Raza's ostrock stood between them, wings and tail outstretched, letting out a call that was answered by the other ostrock. The iridescent tail auras grew brighter, and their matching barrier grew to fully encompass the sorina.

The largest of the two baku was blue with tiger strips and large tusks, one of which was broken halfway down. He was the first to speak.

"Give us the witch!" he bellowed.

Diana took a step back. She turned to Yume.

"Who is that?" she asked.

"That's Daichi," Yume said. "He is the eldest son of Benjiro, the leader of the herd."

Diana turned back to see what was happening. Raza had positioned himself and his ostrock between Daichi and the sorina.

"We have nothing for you here," Raza said sternly.

"We know she is here, we can smell a witch's magic," Daichi roared, "baku are missing, and she's to blame!"

The response of the herd was nearly deafening. They trumpeted and roared in agreement, their billowing smoke growing stronger the angrier they got.

Zane and Diana looked at Yume. Yume's mouth dropped; her brows scrunched in confusion. She looked back at Zane and Diana.

"They think I did something to the baku?" Diana asked, puzzled and frightened.

"This makes no sense," Yume said. "Obviously, it's not you, it's the soothsayer, but what could she possibly want with baku?"

The confrontation between Raza and Daichi continued.

"Give her to us, or we will take her by force!"

"I told you; we don't have anything here for you," Raza replied. "Now move along."

Daichi's smoke poured out, and he made a small leap forward to intimidate Raza. The white ostrock swiped back with its massive talons and snapped at Daichi with its razor-sharp beak. The other baku stepped forward. He was slightly smaller than the other and was shades of green and yellow with Jaguar spots. His tusks were both in tack, and his smoke billowed from his head like a mohawk and down his back to the base of his tail.

"We don't want to harm you," he said firmly. "We just want the girl. We just want answers."

"Eiji, there is no dealing with them," snapped Daichi.

"But brother..." Eiji started.

"In father's absence, I'm in charge," Daichi roared. Smoke shot out of his mane, wrists, and ankles. He turned back to the sorina.

"Find the witch, and bring her to me!"

The other baku started to charge the sorina, knocking against the ostrock's barrier. The harnessed team amped up the barrier as its aura flowed all around them. The mounted ostrock fought back with beaks and talons, trying to keep the baku at bay while the sandmen shifted. They shot pillars of sand at the baku and raised walls as a barricade. The baku in the air slammed down upon the barrier, trying to land on the sorina's deck, while sandmen on the deck helped shift sand.

A group of sandmen on the deck hung back, watching the chaos unfold and over at Diana and her group. The sandmen started talking all at once. Diana, Zane, and Yume turned to see what was happening.

"Why don't we just give them what they want?"

"Yeah, why are we risking ourselves for this bitch?"

"Pitch her over the side!"

The mob moved in towards Diana. Yume leapt in front of Diana. She let out a great warning trumpet from her trunk as she crouched, ready to pounce. Zane took a fighting stance, and a great slab of sand rose behind him, arching over him like a scorpion's tail, ready to strike. Diana activated her dream shield and shimmered away into invisibility.

"Don't take another step," Zane said.

With a quick movement, he shot the sand slab forward a few feet and then back to show he meant business. The mob stopped in their tracks. They looked up at the sand. One reached out in an attempt to shift it away. Zane fought back, slamming the slab down on him, then quickly returning the slab to a striking position.

"Anyone else want to try?"

The sandmen gathered their friend from the floor. Dragging him up, they all hurried away. Zane began to focus on the aerial baku. He sent strike after strike towards them, trying to knock them from the sky.

Yume turned to look at where Daichi and Eiji stood. She leapt over the railing, smoke trailing behind her. Yume landed in the sand and moved to the edge of the barrier that was blocking the other baku from the sorina. She let out a mighty blast from her trunk. The herd stopped to take notice of what was happening.

"That's enough!" she shouted, "she is not the one you want."

"We know a witch took my father and countless other baku, and you defend her? Daichi yelled.

"Brother, she is one of us, hear her out," Eiji said.

"She isn't one of us," Daichi snarled. "Her loyalty is to the sandmen, not to her herd."

"I am a baku," Yume said, smoke billowing. "Your anger is blinding you, Daichi. Benjiro would never lead with rage."

"How dare you speak my father's name while you defend the witch. It's her fault that he's missing."

"Diana had nothing to do with any missing baku," Yume said. "Sandmen are missing too. It seems like it's all being done by the same soothsayer . . ."

"I do not want to hear your stories!" he cried, cutting off Yume.

"Brother, let her finish," Eiji interjected.

"How dare you take the traitor's side?"

"If she has knowledge pertaining to father's disappearance, we owe it to him to hear her out," Eiji turned to Yume. "Please continue."

"Diana is the only one who can bring down the soothsayer. Without her, Sabnare is lost."

"They are most likely working together," Daichi said, "it seems rather strange that for the first time ever, witches enter Sabnare, and they aren't working together. How could they even manage to get here without helping each other? Sabnare is protected from outsiders."

"Zane and I brought Diana here."

"You dare bring an outsider to Sabnare, how foolish are you?"

"She is no outsider; she is the daughter of Warrick and a sandman. Sabnare is just as much a part of her as it is any of us."

Daichi cocked his head, puzzled. Yume stood there holding her ground.

"What kind of fool do you take me for? There are no female sandmen."

"Hey!"

Everyone turned to the sorina. Diana uncloaked herself. She called forth a wave of sand and hopped on. Riding it until it sunk into the ground next to Yume. She faced Daichi, whose body was shaking with rage and billowing smoke.

"You are right I am a witch, but I'm also a sandman, and I'm here to protect Sabnare."

"How can we trust you and be sure you're not the one who took the baku?" Daichi grilled her.

"My father is missing too; I'm looking for answers. All signs point to this soothsayer being the reason for his disappearance. I want the same thing that you do, to find my father and end the threat to Sabnare."

Eiji stepped closer to Diana. He reached out his trunk and sniffed the air around her. Diana knelt down on one knee, extending a hand out to Eiji. He continued to gather her scent as everyone watched.

"Brother, this is not the same scent as the witch who took our father, you can smell the sandman magic mixed in with her witch magic. The witch we smelled before; her magic was pungent with the scent of hatred."

Daichi stepped forward, locking eyes with Diana. He raised his trunk and sniffed the air. He turned his back to Diana.

"She's not the one," Daichi said bitterly. "Let us move on to the castle."

"You can't do that," Yume said.

"Who are you to tell me anything?" Daichi snapped.

"She's right," Diana said. "We need to see exactly what we are up against; we need to slip in unnoticed. If you charge in, who knows how many lives you'll risk."

Daichi began to speak but was cut off by Eiji.

"She is right, brother; I think it's best if we let them go ahead first."

"Fine," snapped Daichi. "We will give you one day before we storm the castle ourselves."

"Thank you, Daichi," said Yume. "We will send word as soon as we find anything."

Daichi glared at Yume. He let out a long, powerful trumpet, swirling away in a puff of smoke. The other baku followed suit, evacuating the area around the sorina. The last baku to leave was Eiji. He gave Diana and Yume a nod before vanishing like the others. Diana and Yume stood in silence for a second.

"You handled that beautifully," Diana said.

"So did you! We make a pretty good team."

Zane made his way down from the sorina, walking over to where Diana and Yume stood.

"Are you both alright?"

"Sorta, this whole thing keeps getting more and more complicated," Diana said.

"What could she possibly need with baku and sandmen?" Yume asked.

"I'm not sure, but we will get to the bottom of it," he said confidently.

Diana certainly hoped so. She watched as the other sandmen checked the sorina for damage and tended to the ostrock. She couldn't shake the feeling that she was being watched. She noticed a robed figure at the back of the sorina. As soon as she saw him, he stepped behind the sorina and out of sight. She hoped it wasn't one of the sandmen from the deck. She knew she needed to be alert and ready.

Zane led them back to the sorina. It wasn't long after they were settled that the sorina continued on its voyage. The group got back to work, flipping through books and scrolls. Diana paged through the spell book from her mother. Hoping that one of the spells could give her a hint as to what the soothsayer could want with baku and sandmen. Nothing in the book gave her any clues. Deep down, she knew it wouldn't. Her mom had handpicked all these spells to cover a variety of conditions. There was nothing that spoke of a situation like that in those pages.

Without even realizing it, she had been rubbing the crystal ball ring that her mother had given her. She stopped and looked at the ring. Her mom said that it could help her see things that were hidden. It was worth a shot. Diana activated the ring, and it grew to its normal size. She focused on the soothsayer, wanting to see what she was up to.

The crystal ball lit up. In the center, pink smoke began to appear and fill the inside. It swirled about until the smoke went white. Diana stared into the smoke, trying to see anything. The smoke swirled back, disappearing into the center as the ball went dark.

"What was that?" asked Yume.

"I tried to use this ring my mom gave me to see the soothsayer, but it didn't work. It just became very cloudy."

"I'd imagine that she'd block the ability to use those," Zane said, "soothsayers have the gift of visions and divination, I'm sure she'd do all she could to block others from using those as a means to watch her."

"That makes sense," Diana said.

Diana looked through her pouches. There had to be an item in there that could help them. She reached in and pulled out the winged scroll from her father. As she pulled it out, the genie bottle fell out on the floor. Zane jumped to his feet.

"Where did you get that?" he asked.

"Phelipe gave it to me. He said he managed to grab it before he escaped the castle."

"Is there a genie inside?" Yume asked.

"I don't think so, he said it was empty. But we can check."

Diana grabbed the bottle, rubbing the side to double-check. Zane and Yume watched with anticipation. She held out the bottle. Nothing happened. Zane's face was full of disappointment.

"Well, it's empty," he said.

"That's too bad a genie could have been helpful," Yume said.

"Wait. An empty genie bottle could be just what we need," Zane said. "We could use the bottle to trap the soothsayer."

"Could that work?" Diana asked. "How do you use an empty genie bottle?"

The winged scroll came to life in her hand. Its wings flapped, and the scroll lowered. The parchment glowed, and an image of a genie bottle appeared on the scroll. Diana swiped through the article on genies. Then she found it. A heading called: how to activate a genie bottle.

To activate a genie bottle. Hold the genie bottle firmly. Look directly at the person you want to imprison in the bottle. Say the word: "Compesco". Once the subject is sucked into the bottle and the topper is resealed, you have a genie.

"This is it," Diana said, "the spell to trap someone as a genie."

She showed the scroll to Zane and Yume. Something didn't feel right. The description was upsetting. She couldn't help thinking that such an ugly practice could happen in such a beautiful place. That genies had been trapped just for being women. She knew this was a completely different circumstance, but it was unsettling just the same.

"This is such wonderful news," Yume cheered.

Diana tried to put on a happy face. They went back to studying the scrolls and journals. Re-energized to look for more information on what to expect and what happened to Warrick. Diana tried to let the motion of the sorina calm her as she pretended to read through a journal while she waited until they arrived at their next stop.

THIRTEEN

The cabin lurched as the sorina came to a stop, sending scrolls sprawling across the floor. Diana collected the rogue scrolls as the sorina's bells started to ring.

"We must have arrived at the oasis," Zane said, standing up.

"What's that?" Diana asked.

"It's a stopping point to let the ostrock rest and drink before continuing on to the castle," he said.

Diana and Yume followed Zane out of their room and onto the deck of the sorina. The sorina was parked on the edge of a small, lush patch of lavender palms. The delightful scent of the lavender tickled Diana's nose as a calm washed over her. Diana looked to see Yume with her eyes closed, taking in the serenity of the oasis. Even Zane's posture was visibly relaxed.

They made their way down to the ground. Following a path that led into the heart of the oasis, Diana looked up in the trees as she walked. The moonlight trickled through the leaves and flowers. White bats with iridescent wings hung from the branches and flew from tree to tree, drinking nectar from the flowers.

The trees parted, revealing a small pool of water as they reached the center of the oasis. The ostrock gathered at its edge, drinking. A few had ventured into the water, intently eyeing something below the surface. One ostrock shot its head underwater and came out with a large metallic-colored fish with coin-like scales in its beak. It threw back its head and, with a few gulps, swallowed the fish.

Diana's stomach rumbled. She hadn't even realized how hungry she was. She had been so focused while working that she had built a mighty appetite.

"Is there anything to eat?" Diana asked. "I'm starving."

"Those men over there are preparing a fire to cook up some trevish," Zane said.

"What's that?"

"Have you ever heard the phrase if wishes were fishes?" he asked. "Whenever someone makes a wish by throwing a coin into a fountain, that wish travels here and turns into a fish that we call a trevish."

How cool. Sabnare was certainly full of surprises. Diana sat with Zane and Yume, joining the other sandmen. The dinner of trevish was delicious. Diana wasn't sure if it was because of how hungry she was, but it was one of the tastiest meals she ever had. She noticed that Yume hadn't had any of the trevish.

"Are you sure you don't want any?"

"Thank you, but baku don't eat food. We eat dreams; we feed on the nightmares of humans."

"I had no idea."

"Yeah, it's part of the balance of Sabnare. It's an intricate lace that is woven and makes the soothsayer's actions even more troubling."

Diana's tilted her head. "What do you mean?"

"When there aren't enough nightmares to feast on, baku have been known to devour hopes and desires."

The idea of people losing their hopes didn't sit well. The increasing gravity of the task at hand weighed heavy on Diana's mind.

Diana finished her dinner and cleared her plate. Some sandmen were cleaning up, while others were laughing and chatting. She gazed into the fire. Watching the flames jump. Listening to the wood crackle as it burned.

A sudden chill ran down Diana's spine. She was overcome by a feeling of being watched again. She turned, facing the trees on the far edge of the oasis. It was hard to make out, but she could have sworn she saw something move. She turned back to the camp to see if anyone else noticed, but no one seemed to. She looked for Zane but couldn't find him.

"Yume, do you know where Zane went?"

Yume looked up at Diana and then surveyed the camp.

"I haven't seen him since he finished his dinner a while ago," Yume replied.

Diana stood up and looked back at the trees. She started to walk towards where she thought she had seen someone.

"Where are you going?" Yume asked.

"I just wanted to check something out," Diana said.

"I'll come with you."

"No, that's okay, wait here I won't be long."

Diana couldn't shake the feeling that someone was following her, but she didn't want to worry Yume. Diana wasn't sure what she was looking for or if there was anything actually there, for that matter. She just needed to clear her mind.

Diana made her way through the trees to the far edge of the oasis that overlooked the Desert of Dreams. She scanned the tree line on both sides. Nothing seemed out of the ordinary for a place that wasn't ordinary. A flash of light in the tree line caught her eye. *Was that someone moon-beaming?* She didn't have time to ponder. The ground began to tremble, with vibrations working up her legs. Causing the sand to stir.

Diana looked on in terror at the sight appearing before her. A giant serpent rose out of the sand. Its large spiked hood blocked out the moonlight, casting Diana in its shadow. The serpent let out a hiss that made her blood run cold. Its patterned hood pulsed and flashed, preparing to strike.

Diana dove out of the way just in time, just missing the glistening fangs. She scrambled to her feet and sprinted into the trees. Running as fast as her feet could carry her, she wove between the tree trunks and jumped over downed logs. The trees splintered and crashed behind her as the serpent pursued. The trees thinned as the clearing came into view.

"Run!" Diana screamed, breaking free of the tree line.

The other sandmen looked up to see trees go flying as the giant serpent crashed through into the clearing.

"Slumbra!" yelled one of the sandmen.

The slumbra hissed as its fangs glistened in the moonlight. The ostrock spooked, running in many directions. Sandmen chased after the flock, attempting to wrangle them.

The slumbra struck. It raised its mighty head, holding the limp, lifeless body of an ostrock in its jaws. The ostrock hung there like a rag doll until the slumbra tossed back its head, swallowing it whole.

"To the sorina!" yelled another sandman.

The sandmen scattered, trying to clear the area. Chaos ensued as some sand-surfed while others moon-beamed and ran. All desperate to escape the slumbra's wrath.

Diana made her way to the end of the oasis, where the sorina was parked. The scene was frantic. Sandmen loaded only what they could carry in their arms. She turned back, trying to see how close the slumbra was. There was no sign of the beast. She couldn't see or hear it. Diana wondered if it was still distracted in the clearing.

The ground trembled, and Diana ran towards the sorina. The slumbra rose from behind the sorina, flashing the pattern on its hood. It lunged towards Diana in a display of power. Its great serpentine body slithered over the top of the sorina. It bared its deadly fangs, dripping with venom. The creature reared, towering above her, ready to strike.

Three pillars of sand collided with the side of the slumbra's head.

A group of three sandmen had launched a defense, shifting the sand. The slumbra whipped its head around, locking onto the sandmen. A swing of its massive tail pummeled into the sandmen, killing them instantly. Their lifeless bodies tumbled through the air. The corpses scattered over the ground, where they dissolved into sand.

With the slumbra distracted, Diana ran. As she picked up speed, she began to sand-surf. The slumbra turned to see her and struck, missing her by inches. She skidded to a stop, spinning around. With an upward motion, Diana shifted a wall of sand. With a swift downward motion, she slammed it down with all the force she could muster onto the slumbra's skull.

The slumbra shook its head as it got up. Its eyes flashed, focusing a hard, cold glare directly at Diana. It reared, preparing to strike again.

Raza and his brilliant white ostrock ran in front of Diana, blocking her. His ostrock screeched and pulled up a barrier. The slumbra struck, repelled by the aura shield. A rage-filled hiss escaped from the slumbra.

"Take cover while we hold it off," Raza said.

Diana hid around the edge of the sorina. She pressed against the wall of the sorina, focusing on their cabin. A swirl of light whisked her away, and she reappeared on the deck of the sorina. It wasn't where she had intended, but it was near the entrance to the corridor where her room was located. She sprinted to the corridor and down the hallway, bursting into her room.

Zane and Yume were nowhere to be found. Diana scrambled to gather all the journals and scrolls that were lying about, loading them into the enchanted pouches. The last thing she grabbed was the enchanted scroll her dad had left her. It sprang to life in her hand. Its wings flapped as the scroll lowered. She began to swipe through it.

"Where's the entry about slumbras?" she asked out loud in her panic.

The scroll began to flip through pictures at an impressive rate until a picture of a slumbra appeared. Just as she was about to read the entry, there was a thunderous crash. The whole sorina shook. Diana found herself on the ground. The roof of the sorina had been ripped off with one mighty swing of the slumbra's tail.

"Dream Shield!" Diana cried out as she tried to block her face from the splintering debris that was raining down on her. The slumbra's tail came crashing down. The far wall crumbled, revealing the front half of the sorina. The slumbra had split it in two on its first strike.

Diana could see flashes of the slumbra as it was attacking other sandmen. The slumbra sped around the back of the sorina, chasing after something. Diana's half of the sorina shook as the slumbra crashed into it. Diana stumbled and lost her footing. She slipped over the edge where the wall used to be into the canyon between the two halves of the sorina.

Diana spun through the air as she plummeted to the ground. She saw her scroll still flying there, glowing and flashing. She continued to spin and was now facing the ground. Diana curled up behind the shield the best she could, closing her eyes preparing for impact.

Diana felt a force impact her from the side. She was no longer falling but was now hurtling sideways. She opened her eyes. Zane was carrying her in his arms as he sand-surfed her out of the split sorina. Once they were not directly in harm's way, he slowed down and set her down.

"Oh my god, Zane, you're okay," she cried, hugging him.

"No one is okay yet," he said, "we need to take care of this slumbra."

As if the slumbra had heard its name, it raised its head over the side of the sorina. It zeroed in on Zane and Diana. With a blood-curdling hiss, it charged. It slammed through the sorina, further collapsing it and sending its halves farther apart. Its gaze never faltered as it headed right for them. The slumbra leaped up and dove underground.

"Watch out. Who knows where it will come up," Zane said.

Zane shifted the sand and began to ride a tall wave. Diana put away her shield and followed suit. They both stood on tall pillars of sand, surveying the area. The slumbra breached the surface behind them. Zane and Diana sand-surfed in opposite directions in an attempt to confuse the beast. Zane and Diana's movements were very much in harmony. They sand-surfed back and forth in opposite directions. When their paths crossed, one would go high and the other low.

Zane shot javelins of sand at the slumbra. Diana shifted sand at it, too, but with nowhere near the ability of Zane. Diana was lucky she was doing alright while sand-surfing on its own.

The slumbra lunged for Diana. A spike on its crest caught her as she tried to get out of the way. Diana lost control of the sand beneath her and plummeted to the ground.

The slumbra circled back to face her. Zane sped in, blasting the slumbra with sand. It let out an enraged hiss. With a swift flick of its tail, it caught Zane in the leg and knocked him off of his feet. The slumbra turned back to Diana. It slithered closer, stretching its crest to make itself look as large as possible. It erratically flashed its patterns and hissed as it went in for the kill.

A puff of pink smoke appeared and slammed directly into the side of the slumbra's head. The smoke cleared, revealing Yume hovering in the air, a cloud of smoke surrounding her ankles.

"Yume, be careful!" Diana shouted.

The enraged slumbra glared at Yume. Its tail shot up and wrapped around her. It constricted on Yume as she screamed, then promptly passed out. The slumbra brought the baku to its face. It tilted back its great head and opened its mouth. It raised its tail above its mouth.

"No!" Diana shouted.

Diana stood up. A great purple energy surged around her. The slumbra paused momentarily, looking at Diana before returning to its snack. It repositioned Yume above its gaping mouth.

"I said NO!"

Diana's eyes glowed purple as she raised a hand towards the Slumbra. A blast of fire shot from her hand, severing the tail that held Yume.

Yume fell to the ground. Zane, from his position, raised the sand to meet her and cushion her fall. Zane tried to stand, but he couldn't. He looked over to Diana. Her eyes glowed purple with rage. Her body bathed in a shimmering purple energy that Zane had never seen.

The slumbra bellowed in pain. It sped across the sand towards Diana, leaving a trail of blood behind it.

Diana took to a wave of sand and began to surf. The power surged inside her, fueling her. It was as if someone had taken control of her body. The magic controlled her actions like a puppeteer. She shot a stream of flames at the slumbra and missed, melting the sand and leaving a jagged line of purple glass.

Diana continued to wildly throw flames at the creature as it pursued her. Shooting from her hands like ninja stars, sizzling the flesh of the slumbra with each hit. Scaring the desert with each miss. The slumbra's scales gave it some protection from the flames, as scorch marks marred its body. Her eyes continued to glow as the intensity of her attack increased.

They circled the broken remains of the sorina in a standoff. The slumbra would strike, and Diana would shoot her flames. Diana tried to lose the Slumbra between the halves of the sorina. It shot out of the sand behind her, leaping over her head and diving back into the sand.

The bleeding stump of the slumbra's tail knocked Diana's scroll from the air, where it had been floating and flashing. The scroll landed next to the shredded hull of the sorina and where the slumbra had returned underground.

Diana rose into the air, perched high above the sorina. She could feel every grain of sand around her and how it moved. She now sensed the slumbra's movements underground. She focused on its movements, trying to predict where it would breach the surface again.

She held her hands in front of her, conjuring a great fireball between them. Her eyes glowed with increasing intensity. The flames turned purple as the fireball expanded between her hands.

The slumbra breached the surface, towering over the sand. Its mouth was gaping, ready to attack. Diana raised the fireball above her head and thrust it down at the slumbra, followed by another smaller fireball behind it. The purple fireball went right into the slumbra's mouth, barreling down its throat. The slumbra hardened as it crystallized into jagged purple glass. The second fireball hit, following the same path, shattering the crystal almost as quickly as it was formed.

Diana's eyes stopped glowing, and the aura around her dissipated. The sand beneath her gave way, settling back into the ground. Diana's eyes closed as she passed out. Her limp, depleted body falling back to the ravaged oasis.

CHAPTER

FOURTEEN

The pounding in her head was all Diana could hear as she struggled to open her eyes. She blinked a couple of times, trying to clear her vision. Her eyes burned. Billowing smoke filled the air, making it even more difficult. The sorina was engulfed in dancing flames. Out of the flames and smoke, a shadowy figure appeared, walking towards Diana. Their face clouded by the smokey air.

"Zane?" she asked, squinting and reaching out a hand.

The figure bent down, keeping their face obscure beneath their hood. They reached for her scroll that was lying a few feet from where she woke up. Purple lightning shot from the scroll's encrusted gems, zapping the figure as they placed their hand on the scroll. Their body convulsed, screaming, as the magic surged over them. Stumbling back, the figure vanished in a blinding flash of light.

Diana blinked several more times; her vision started to come back into focus. She crawled over to the scroll, tucking it away safely in her robes. Fighting through her pain, she stood back up, scanning the flaming wreckage.

"Zane! Yume!" she called out.

Diana surveyed the sand, finding no sign of either of them. She shifted the sand beneath her, raising her to a better viewing position. From her new vantage point, she saw something moving in the distance.

Diana sand-surfed over to the moving figure. As she got closer, she saw it was Yume. Diana sped up, moving as fast as she could control. Her sand wave came down, rejoining the rest of the desert, placing Diana next to Yume.

"Diana, help him," Yume said, tears in her eyes.

Next to Yume was Zane. He was lying unconscious, covered up to his neck in sand. Carefully, Diana shifted the sand off him, like pulling off a blanket. Uncovering his leg revealed a mangled mess.

Tears welled in Diana's eyes. She dropped to her knees beside him. Her hands reached out over him, shaking, afraid to touch him, not knowing what to do to help. There was no one left around to help her. All the others fled or were killed when the slumbra attacked.

What should I do? What could I do?

Diana suddenly remembered the spell book from her mother. She dug through her robes, retrieving her spell book. Frantically flipping through the pages, she came across a healing spell. She looked over the spell, and it required the use of her wand. She dug into her robes and pulled out the wand. The book said to activate the wand and then create blue and green ripples of healing energy.

Diana concentrated her energy on the end of the wand. She made a swirl in the air, and the tip of the wand dimly lit. She focused on the tip, and it began to glow bright blue. Diana passed the wand over Zane's leg, willing the wand's energy to ripple.

The energy released from the wand in sharp blasts. Each blast jerked Zane's leg into a new position with a stomach-turning crack.

Zane woke up screaming in pain. Diana tried the spell again. Two more bursts from the wand resulted in two more cracks as Zane's leg tried to contort itself back to its original form. Zane's eyes rolled back in his head, passing back out from the pain.

"Diana, calm down and focus," Yume said. "You can do this."

Diana held the wand in front of her. She focused on the glowing tip of the wand. She closed her eyes while keeping the wand in her mind's eye. She shut out all that was around her, the crackling of the burning sorina, the sooty smell of smoke in the air. All there was was her and the wand. She pictured the wand gently pulsing between blue and green. Then she envisioned the energy slowly rippling out.

Diana opened her eyes. The wand was doing exactly what she had wanted. She slowly passed the wand over Zane. Instinctively, she started at his head, letting the energy fall over him, moving down his body. She reached his leg and continued. She moved slowly, and the rippling intensified. His leg began to gently correct itself as the wand's energy washed over it.

Zane's leg was now in place, and she moved back up, holding the wand over his chest. The blue and green energy cascaded down while diminishing in strength until the light went out, and the last of the energy settled into Zane's body.

Diana and Yume waited for any sign that the spell had worked. They sat there, still, with bated breath. Zane's eyes flickered as his body began to stir. His purple eyes sparkled in the moonlight as he looked at Diana and Yume.

"You're okay!" Yume shouted, wrapping her trunk around his head while tears streamed down her face. Zane began to sit up. Diana took his hand to help.

"Do you think you can stand?" Diana asked.

"Yeah, I think so," he said.

With the help of Diana and Yume, Zane shakily rose to his feet. He looked over at the sorina. The burning wreckage sat in the middle of a desolate landscape, littered with purple shards of glass spikes rising from the sand. The splintered remains of lavender palms were strewn about. The oasis was unrecognizable.

"What happened?" Yume asked as she looked at the destruction before her.

"I'm not sure. It's all pretty fuzzy to me," Diana said, rubbing her temple.

"It was Diana," Zane said.

"Me?"

"Yes. Magic is controlled by our emotions. When Yume was in danger, it blinded you, and your magic took over. In your rage, you conjured fire. It destroyed the slumbra and left these glass crystals in the sand."

Diana couldn't believe her ears. *I did all this?* She could barely remember it happening. She looked at all the damage before her. Her stomach turned, knowing that this was all because of her.

"What I don't understand is why there was a slumbra here," Yume said, "this isn't its normal territory."

"My guess is that someone led it here. Someone who didn't want us to make it to the castle," Zane said.

The idea that someone had sent the slumbra rattled Diana. *Who could have done this?* Then she remembered the flash of light at the edge of the oasis and the shrouded figure when she woke.

"When I first came to, there was someone there," Diana said. "I couldn't make out who it was. They tried to take my scroll, but it zapped them away. Do you think they've alerted the castle that we are on our way?"

"I'm not sure. But we will need to take more precautions and make our next moves as if they know we are on the way," he said.

"What should we do?" Yume asked.

"First off, let's try and remove as much evidence of what happened here as we can," he said. "Yume, if you can work on clearing the smoke, Diana and I will work on putting out the flames."

Yume flew towards the smoking wreckage. Zane and Diana followed behind. Zane shifted a stream of sand and focused it at the base of the flames. Diana followed suit. Yume flew around the smoke like a dog herding sheep.

Yume used her trunk to suck up smoke as she ran through the air. When she could no longer take in any more, she dispelled it with the smoke that sparkled out from her feet. Zane had managed to gain more control over the flames on his side of the sorina. Diana upped the pressure of her sand stream, and the flames began to recede.

The group's collaborative effort managed to disperse the smoke and extinguish the flames. They stood there looking at the charred husk of what used to be a sorina in what used to be a serene retreat.

"We need to bury it," Zane said.

"Do you think we can?" Diana asked.

"We don't have any choice. We want as little evidence of our mission as possible or that we were here at all."

Zane reached over and took Diana's hand into his own. She looked at her hand in his and back to the wreckage that stood before him. Diana felt the hairs on the back of her neck raise as Zane's energy began to harmonize with her own. Zane raised his hands in the air without releasing his grip. Diana followed along with her other arm.

Without words, she knew what they had to do. Their magic swirled together in beautiful temperance. His magic led the way, and her magic followed, strengthening his.

Sand began to swirl around the sorina, counter-clockwise rising up and outward. Slowly, without words, they began to lower their hands in unison. The ground began to shake as the broken halves of the sorina sank into the whirlpool of sand. The sand began to close up over where the sorina had been, leaving no trace of it.

The last grains of sand settled as they released their hands. Their energy no longer danced together but pulled back like a vacuum. They stood there. Alone. Together.

Zane lowered himself to the ground and took a seat. Diana and Yume joined him.

Diana's chest rose and fell with labored breath. Yume curled up, taking long, purposeful breaths. Diana noticed her normal pink and purple hue had become slightly gray in tone.

Diana looked over the desolate oasis. Splintered trees and jagged purple glass stood as a reminder that she didn't have full control over her powers. If she couldn't get a handle on her magic, she worried that she would let everyone down, but mostly herself.

FIFTEEN

After a short rest, they continued making their way to the castle. Zane led the group, sand-surfing ahead. Diana followed, with Yume flying behind. Still drained from the events at the oasis, they pushed forward. Diana was so focused on sand-surfing that she nearly crashed into Zane as he stopped ahead of her. He crouched behind a large dune while Yume landed next to him.

"What is it?" Diana asked.

Zane motioned with his head. Diana turned to look. Nothing could have prepared her for what met her eyes.

Standing there in front of her was a magnificent castle made of sand. A large outer wall stood on the edge of a moat, surrounding the castle. From the dune, they could see over the wall and into a spacious courtyard. The castle had many large towers reaching up to meet the night sky. Several bridges and stairways connected different parts of the castle. Rising higher than any other was the central tower. Sitting above it was a large purple diamond. The moons' light sparkled through its many facets as it peacefully spun.

"Whoa," was all Diana could muster and all that felt appropriate.

"That's the Diamond of Dreams," Zane said, pointing at the diamond. "That is the source of all the dream sand in Sabnare."

The diamond held such beauty and power. The importance of the diamond left Diana humbled in its presence. It was hard to look away. Watching the Diamond of Dreams brought her a sense of calm that she had not felt since arriving in Sabnare.

A sudden movement caught Diana's attention. A tawny-colored owl shot out of one of the tower windows. The owl circled the castle, gaining altitude.

A smile spread across Diana's face, watching the owl fly. Then she saw the look on the faces of her companions. Zane's whole body stood rigid. The brightness of Yume's eyes was gone. Replaced by a look of apprehension. Neither of them took their eyes off the owl. The owl climbed higher. Now, above the castle. Circling the Diamond of Dreams. It began its final approach for a landing on top of the diamond.

A pulse of energy shot out of the Diamond of Dreams. The owl screeched as it was blasted back, crackling with purple energy. The owl plummeted toward the ground in front of the castle wall. Its body spun wildly in the air as it fell.

The ground was quickly rising to meet the owl. The air swooshed as the owl's wings opened, reorienting itself. Wings spread, it slowed its descent and went to land on the ground.

All of a sudden, its wings grew larger. Its legs grew to meet the ground. With a final spin, it finished its transformation. What were its wings now was a light cloak. Wrapped around a woman. A witch. Diana couldn't make out her face from the distance, but she knew she had finally laid eyes on the soothsayer.

The group stayed crouched down behind the dune. Allowing themselves to peak over enough to keep watching the scene unfold.

The soothsayer raised her glowing hands and made a motion above her head. Dark shadowy figures began to rise from the sand and surrounded her. They looked like humans made out of darkness, except for their glowing white eyes and practically featureless faces.

The soothsayer shouted angrily at the shadowy figures, making a gesture with a glowing hand. They turned away and headed back toward the desert. Disappearing back into the sand.

"What are those things?" Diana asked.

"Those are dreamons," Zane replied.

"They form when there's an abundance of dream energy not being utilized," Yume chimed in.

Diana watched as the last dreamon disappeared. The soothsayer looked up at the Diamond of Dreams and then stormed off into the castle.

"What do we do now?" Diana asked.

"We need to carefully enter the castle's courtyard," Zane said.

"How are we going to do that?" Yume chimed in.

"We will need to go invisible and move quickly through the courtyard."

"I can't go invisible," Yume said nervously.

"We can cloak you as long as we are making physical contact," Zane reassured her, returning his attention to the entrance of the castle.

Yume let out a sigh of relief. Diana continued watching the castle.

"How long should we wait?" Diana asked.

"Just a moment longer to be sure the courtyard is clear," Zane said.

The anticipation was killing her. Diana wondered what would be awaiting them once they entered the castle. All that she knew was that she needed to be smart and face things head-on.

CHAPTER

SIXTEEN

Zane led Diana and Yume to the entrance of the castle. Cloaked with invisibility, they moved with haste so as not to draw attention to themselves. The group crossed the castle's threshold and entered an expansive courtyard.

The courtyard reminded Diana of the oasis. Open space, with a few lavender palms sporadically placed along its perimeter. A stream ran through its center, flanked by grates on each side that let the water flow freely. A tiny wooden bridge stood over the center of the stream, leading to the main part of the castle.

Zane confirmed that the coast was clear, quickly escorting everyone over to the right towards a small building. The building was positioned against the wall and stretched from the entrance to where the stream entered the courtyard. Standing in front of the door, Zane took a last look around the courtyard to see if anyone was around. Confidant that the coast was clear, he took out a key. With a swift movement, he opened the door and ushered them inside. Zane quickly locked the door, securing themselves inside.

"Where are all the baku?" Yume asked.

"It is strange," Zane replied.

"What is?" Diana asked.

"The castle's courtyard is usually full of activity and baku," Zane said. "I've never seen the courtyard be completely absent of baku and sandmen."

Diana could see the worry all over Yume's face. She turned to Zane.

"So, what should we do?"

"Let's take a look around your father's chamber and see if there are any clues as to what happened to him."

The three of them spread out, searching the different areas of the chamber for anything that might be of use. It reminded Diana of his place in the village but set up more like an office. There were bookshelves full of scrolls across every wall. Yume scoured the bookshelves while Zane inspected the desk.

Diana entered the bedroom and opened the drawers of a large dresser. She found extra robes and a plethora of items that she couldn't identify. Nothing that seemed like it could give them any answers. She walked over to the bed that sat against the wall. Next to it was a nightstand.

Diana opened the drawer. Nothing out of the ordinary. She moved aside bits of fabric and string, along with a few candles. Towards the back, her fingers ran over a rough burlap pouch. Diana pulled out the pouch. It was full of dream sand. She decided to attach it next to the pouch she already had in case the need for it were to arise.

As Diana went to attach it, something caught her eye. A crystal that had been stuck to the bottom of the bag had freed itself. She watched as it hit the ground with a horrific crash, breaking into three pieces. She dropped down to gather the pieces.

Diana tried fitting the jagged pieces back together like a puzzle. She held the pieces of the crystal together as Zane entered the room. He looked at the crystal protruding from Diana's hands.

"Is that a dream shard?" he asked, unable to hide his shock.

"I don't know. I mean, maybe it was, I'm not sure," she replied.

"What do you mean, was?" he asked, suspicion dripping from his voice.

Diana lowered the crystal to the floor. She then pulled the ends away from the center, revealing the damage. The color drained from Zane's face when he saw what had become of the dream shard.

"It was an accident," she stammered, "I didn't even know it was there when it shattered."

Diana had never seen such a look on Zane's face. Normally calm and unreadable. He was clearly at a loss.

"What are dream shards?" Diana asked.

Zane took a deep breath. He closed his eyes while he let the words form in his mind.

"Dream shards are the remnants of the most powerful and inspiring dreams of mankind," he said, "and sometimes they hold the visions from people's prophetic dreams."

Diana had no idea that it was so important. She looked at the damage before her. Guilt sprung on her like a coiled serpent.

"Is it fixable?" she asked hopefully.

"I don't know," Zane replied, "I've never known this to happen before."

Before Diana could say another word, Yume came bounding in.

"You need to come quick," she said, "something major is happening in the courtyard."

Diana hastily put the pieces of the dream shard in a pouch inside her robes. She rushed down the hallway after Yume and Zane. As they reached the door, they could hear the commotion outside.

"What should we do?" Diana asked.

"We need to sneak out there so we can find out what's going on," Zane said.

"How are we going to do that?" Yume asked.

"Yume, we need you to stay here," Zane said, "We need to be able to maneuver quickly and won't be able to keep you invisible."

Yume began to protest but quickly relented. She knew Zane was right.

"Diana, we will go invisible, and you should use your dream catcher shield," he said, "but focus on it shielding us from perception."

"Dream shield!"

The dream catcher sprang to life, leaping from Diana's hip into the air. Spinning faster and faster, growing larger with each rotation. It stopped growing, and its center began to glow purple. As it spun, the light spread to the outer edges, growing brighter and more intense. The dream shield let out a final flash like a strobe light. As the light faded from view, so did the shield. All that was left was a ghostly spinning silhouette.

Zane cracked open the door with care, not making a sound. At Diana's command, the shield slipped out the small opening of the door. It moved into place, spinning and hovering in front of the door.

Zane opened the door wider, going invisible as he slipped out. Diana followed him, fading from view, anxious to see what awaited them in the courtyard.

Crouching behind the shield, Diana's heart sank at the scene unfolding before her. A large group of dreamon had returned. They moved around the courtyard like a depressive koi pond. Their howling was loud and chaotic. As they circled, Diana caught glimpses of what was in the center.

Three dreamon had a sandman in their grasp. He was putting up a good fight, grunting with rage and fatigue. Several other dreamon were restraining two baku and another sandman, who didn't seem to be fairing as well as the first sandman. The baku's terrified squeals and yelling sandmen mixed with the storm of dreamon howls, creating a crescendo of terror.

An ear-piercing screech came from overhead. Diana and Zane watched as an owl flew out from the tower and dove straight down towards the dreamon. It pulled up a few feet above the ground and began to circle, herding the dreamon like a sheepdog. With each pass, the hoard of dreamon began to settle.

The owl flew over to the other side of the stream closest to the castle's main gate. It veered up as it prepared to land. Its body began to melt and shift. Its wings transfigured into flowing garb while its limbs stretched and contorted as it returned to its true form. The soothsayer.

Diana finally got a good look at the soothsayer as she adjusted her robes and skirt. She appeared to be in her fifties, with brown eyes and light brown shoulder-length curly hair.

The dreamons' howling had subsided as they waited restlessly for the soothsayer to speak. The captive sandman and baku, tired and weak, looked upon the soothsayer with apprehension. The soothsayer took slow, purposeful steps towards the hoard. Inching ever closer.

"Delfina!" a voice shouted. "What is the meaning of this?"

An ornery-looking bald sandman came tromping out of the castle's towers. His white mustache and beard popped against his deep olive skin. His dull purple eyes sunken into his wrinkled face.

"What do you want, Malvin?" She turned to look at him, clearly perturbed.

"Don't give me that!" he shouted. "This is not part of our deal."

The soothsayer let out a laugh as if she were the hostess of a dinner party. She smiled,

"My dear Malvin, if you had been doing an acceptable job, I wouldn't have to take matters into my own hands." She motioned with her arm to the scene before them. "This is nothing more than a show of your incompetence."

Malvin began to speak. Delfina raised a hand to silence him.

"I don't want to hear it."

She began walking through the hoard of dreamon.

"Our deal, Malvin, is for me to regain that which was stolen from me. Then I will leave this world, and you will be in charge of running it however you see fit. And until that time, if you are incapable of providing me what I need." She reached out and delicately held the face of one of the captive sandmen, looking him in the eye. "I will take it by any means necessary."

She dropped the terrified sandman's face. She strode back to where Malvin stood.

"That last sandman you sent me wasn't fully secured and escaped before I could finish."

"Phelipe's escape wasn't my fault," Malvin protested.

"All I know is that he's gone, and I still need more," Delfina hissed. "Once I get what I want, you'll get what you want, and not a moment before."

She turned back to the hoard. "Why are you still standing here, take them away."

The dreamon began moving towards the castle. The sandmen and baku cried out as the dreamon dragged them away, disappearing into the bowels of the castle.

Delfina turned to Malvin once more.

"I'm glad to have you as an ally so that I can do my work undetected, but let me make this clear. You are still here because I allow it. If you continue to fail me or to question me." She paused for effect. "Then I will sever our ties and continue alone. Do I make myself clear?"

"Perfectly," Malvin snarled.

Delfina looked up at the tower. She lifted her arms, bringing the fabric of her cloak with her as she began shifting. The familiar shape of an owl began to take form, and Delfina took to the air and returned to the tower window that she had appeared from.

Malvin stood for a moment, watching Delfina return to the tower. A scowl spread over his already uninviting face. When she was out of sight, he trudged back to the castle, leaving the courtyard empty except for Diana and Zane.

Zane nudged Diana and returned to the entrance of Warrick's chambers. They let down their invisibility as they stepped through the door, securing it behind them. Diana returned the dream catcher to its regular form and put it away on her hip.

Yume was waiting for them by the door.

"What happened out there?" she asked.

"A group of dreamon captured a group of baku and sandmen and brought them back to the castle," Diana said.

Yume's eyes went wide, "what happened then?"

"The soothsayer appeared, and then she was confronted by Malvin," Diana said.

"Was he able to help them?" Yume asked.

"Malvin has been helping the soothsayer," Zane interjected.

"What, that can't be! Why would he do such a thing?"

"It's no secret that he has very specific views on how things should work in Sabnare. He must think helping her will give him more control."

Diana let the words sink in. "Do you think Malvin could be responsible for my dad's disappearance?"

Zane saw the worry in her eyes. "I honestly don't know. I don't think Malvin would outright target Warrick. Everyone knows that they don't see eye to eye all the time, but it seems too sloppy. We know that Warrick knew something was happening and was preparing for it."

"So, what do we do now?" Diana asked.

Zane thought for a moment before responding. "I think I should head to the dungeons to try and take inventory of the situation."

"I think I'm going to stay here; I think I have figured out how Warrick has his journals and scrolls organized, and I'd love to see what I can find," Yume said.

"That will be very helpful," Zane replied.

"And what should I do?" Diana asked.

Before anyone could answer, her father's scroll flew out of Diana's robes and opened. It hovered there in midair, its wings beating mightily. The scroll began to reveal an image.

"That's the castle layout," Zane said.

The scroll showed where they were, complete with three glowing orbs showing where Diana, Zane, and Yume were standing. Then, a spot on one of the towers was highlighted. Diana tapped the spot, and the image changed to that of a room full of crystals.

"That's the Library of Dreams," Zane said. "It's where we house the greatest dreams of mankind, prophetic dreams, and any other important dreams. It's wall-to-wall dream shards."

Diana reached into her pouch and removed the dream shard that she had found in her father's drawer.

"Is there a way to view the dreams?"

"There is a viewing pedestal in the center of the library that can allow you to view the dreams."

"I think it wants you to see what's on the shard," Yume said.

Diana looked at the scroll. She watched as it bobbed gently in midair, its wings fluttering. She assumed her father must have set it up to lead her there, hoping that she had found the shard.

"There must be a reason that he was keeping this shard hidden away and not in the library," Diana said. "I think I should go check it out."

"Will you be okay going alone?" Zane asked. The concern was all over his face.

"I think so," she said. "The scroll will show me the way. Plus, it looks like it shows where people are located. It had markers for the three of us standing in this room."

"Are you sure, I could go with you if you'd like," Yume said.

"I appreciate the offer," she said, "but you're so close to figuring out his journals. We really need you to focus on that."

"If you say so," Yume said. It was apparent that she wasn't entirely convinced, considering the last time Diana went off on her own, a slumbra attacked.

"We all know what we have to do," Diana said.

"Let's head out and meet back here as quickly as possible," said Zane.

With Yume pouring over Warrick's journals, Diana and Zane left the chamber, all three of them hoping to find answers.

SEVENTEEN

Diana cautiously made her way towards the library. She navigated through the halls, following the floating scroll as it led the way. The castle's hallways were illuminated by glowing purple crystals that lined the floor and ceiling where they met the walls. Meticulous carvings adorned the sandy walls. Delicately stitched tapestries hung at different intervals and were as numerous and varied as people's dreams. Several had dragons; others featured baku. Some portrayed what she assumed to be noteworthy sandmen. There were scenes depicting genies, ostrock, and even cat creatures. Several had other creatures she couldn't identify. Even a slumbra made an appearance. *Shudder*.

Under different circumstances, she would've stopped to appreciate how incredible and beautiful the castle was. She wished she could take it all in, but the scroll pressed relentlessly forward, wings fluttering away, leading her up a spiraling staircase in a tower.

The scroll stopped before reaching the entrance to the next hallway. She could see on the map two orbs making their way down the hall. Diana exhaled and let herself go invisible. She pressed herself and the scroll against the wall, hoping they weren't heading for the staircase.

The sound of shuffling footsteps filled the sand-coated corridor. She held her breath. Two sandmen entered the stairwell. Diana's heart raced, and the hairs on her arms stood on end. The sandmen made their way up the stairs and away from where she was standing.

She stood a bit longer, listening intently, being sure they had passed. Diana let out a sigh of relief. The scroll returned to its place, flying in front of her. The map showed that the coast was clear, and the scroll continued out into the hall.

The scroll led Diana a bit farther down a hallway until it stopped at a large wooden double door. She reached her hand out. The warmth of the wood was inviting to the touch. Diana double-checked that it was the right place on the map and pushed on the door. The heavy door let out a creek as it slowly slid open. Diana stopped. She hoped no one heard the sound of the door. She checked the scroll. No one in sight. Just her marker glowing on the map. She gave the door another push and slipped in when the opening was just large enough to fit through. The sight before her was far beyond her greatest expectation.

The Library of Dreams was massive. It was a large rectangular-shaped room the size of a football field and several stories tall. Each level encircled the room with shelves filled with dream shards. Hanging across the center of the room were more tapestries secured from the third level on opposite sides. The ceiling was a glassed-in atrium style that allowed the light of the moons and stars to filter in. The central tower of the castle rose above, overlooking the library. The Diamond of Dreams, slightly spinning above it, glinting in the moonlight.

Diana closed the door as much as she could without making too much noise. To a casual observer, no one should notice it. Hopefully, it would also allow her to hear if anyone approached.

She made her way towards a large wooden pedestal that sat in the center of the room. On its front sat a plaque that read:

Here, we house the greatest dreams of mankind. May the energy of these dreams continue to inspire future dreams.

Its top had three large crystals sticking out from the top. They sat equidistant from each other. One was red, another blue and the last green. Three small clear crystals sat between each, leading from one color to the next, almost like the face of a clock. In the center, there was an opening.

The scroll showed an image; the first was of the dream viewer. The next image showed a dream shard being placed in the center. The next showed that the red, green, and blue crystals needed to be pushed down in that specific order to activate the pedestal and view the dream.

Diana reached into her robes and pulled out the pieces of the dream shard. She looked at the pieces in her hands and the dream viewer. She wondered how it was going to work with it being broken. She lined up the pieces, holding them together, and placed one tip into the dream viewer's center. Carefully, she pushed down on the shard until she could feel it lock in place. Luckily, it went deep enough that the pieces could rest on top of each other. Just the top part of the crystal was visible, while the other parts were safely tucked away inside.

"Okay, let's hope this works," she said to herself.

Diana reached for the red crystal, pressing it down until it locked into place. Next, she did the same with the green one. That only left the blue crystal. It stood there above all the other crystals. This was the last piece. This could reveal all the answers. She hoped it would work. It had to work. With care, she locked the last crystal into place.

Nothing happened. Diana looked over the dream viewer, looking for anything that could be off. She consulted the scroll to be sure she followed the steps correctly. Before she could check anything else, the viewer sprang to life.

The dream shard in the center began to spin. It picked up speed, and then the red crystal lit up. One by one, the crystals began to glow in a clockwise manner. Then, a flash of green, followed by the next three clear crystals. Blue was the final of the colored crystals to come to life. Then, the last of the clear crystals lit, completing the circle.

A pillar of light shot up through the center, illuminating the dream shard. Beams shot out from the red, green, and blue crystals. They met in the center, creating a pyramid of light. A flash came from the clear crystals as their light shot out from the dream viewer to illuminate the room. The light swirled and intensified until, with a final flash, the room disappeared before her eyes.

It was as if Diana had stepped into some type of void. She couldn't make out the floors, walls, or ceiling. There was nothing but light. Images began to slowly form. A scene was beginning to take shape.

The images kept jumping in and out, like a television that was having trouble with its signal. Diana was struggling to make sense of it all. The scenes appeared, some parts clearer than others. The sound was garbled with moments of clarity. Images of fighting and unrest filled the area, including an old woman hitting a car with her cane from a crosswalk, then faded away. Two new figures began to appear. Diana couldn't make out the first, but the second was clear as day. It was Delfina.

Delfina pleaded with the other figure and began yelling. Diana struggled to make out what was being said. She thought that she had heard the word gift from Delfina and the word daughter from the unknown figure.

The scene was replaced by a crazed Delfina leading a dreamon attack on sandmen. It appeared to be a large battle. The images came faster now and were harder to decipher. Until a final image came into view. Delfina seemed to be connected to the Diamond or Dreams. Then the scene flashed again, showing the Diamond of Dreams exploding.

The world around her began swirling away faster and faster. Then, with a whoosh that almost made her lose her balance, all the light returned to the center of the dream viewer. The library was back in view, and the crystals on the dream viewer were slowly beginning to dim as the dream shard was slowly coming to a stop.

Diana was trying to process all that she had seen when she heard voices coming from the hallway. She stealthily made her way to the door so she could listen. She checked the scroll as it brought back up the map. It showed two dots on the other side of the doorway.

Malvin's voice was easily recognized, even being muffled by the mostly closed door. His anger was palpable. She inched her way closer to the crack in the door so she could hear better.

"Things better have worked out the way you said they did," Malvin bellowed, "I won't tolerate any more surprises."

The sound of muffled footsteps passed through the cracked open door. Diana checked the scroll, one of the dots charged off while the other was still outside. She took a few steps, backing away from the door.

Without warning, the dream viewer expelled the dream shard, sending the fragments flying up into the air, clanging against each other as they fell to the ground.

Diana ran over to collect the pieces. Hoping the noise hadn't been heard. As she crouched down, grabbing the fragments, she heard a sound. The great wooden door to the library was creaking open. Diana dove behind a row of shelves, followed by the scroll. She went invisible. Peering out through the space between shelves, she watched as someone entered the room.

Diana's heart pounded in her ears as a sandman entered the room. The sandman lowered his hood, scanning the room. Her stomach fell, Diana couldn't believe her eyes. There, standing in front of her, was Tario.

"Hello," he called out, "anyone in here?"

Diana's heart raced. She looked around, trying to figure out her next move. The scroll showed the library's floor plan. She kept going back and forth between the two when she noticed, although subtle, her footprints on the sandy floor.

She reached out her hand. Tario was looking on the other side of the room. She gently shifted the sand, removing the traces of her footprints.

Tario continued working his way through the library. Diana was focused on the door. She crept along the shelf, keeping low. She needed a distraction to draw Tario far enough away so that she could slip out the doorway.

Tario had reached the dream viewer, running his fingers across the surface as he scanned the room. Looking at the upper floors. Checking the ground. Diana referenced the scroll's floor plan. She decided to focus on the back corner farthest from her. She wondered if she could channel her shift so that it would look like she had sand-surfed in that direction. If she was going to try, she had to time it just right. Diana needed Tario to just see the tail end of the sand's movement.

Diana waited. Anticipating Tario's moves. He turned, and Diana moved. A warmth rippled across her body as she pushed forward with her arms. Shifting the sand towards the back of the library, turning behind a shelf. Tario finished his scan just in time.

"Stop!" he yelled.

Tario ran towards the shelves, lifting up a wall of sand to block off that area as he did. Diana took her chance and leapt out from behind the shelves. She dashed towards the open door.

Slam! A wave of sand crashed against the door, blocking her exit. Before she could even process it, a pillar of sand rose up and knocked her across the room, spilling out the contents of her pouches on the floor by the door.

"I thought the slumbra would have been enough to finish you off," Tario said.

Diana rose to her feet. Eyes locked on Tario; she took a slow, purposeful step.

"You brought the slumbra?"

Tario smirked. "Of course I did," he laughed.

Diana held her stance, looking for an opportunity. She knew that she needed to distract him.

"Why would you do that? I thought you were keeping a lookout at the village."

"That's what I wanted you to think."

"But I trusted you . . . Zane trusted you."

Tario's face flinched at the mention of Zane's name. His gaze wandered down to the floor. Diana took the moment and made a break for the door. Sand-surfing across the floor. Tario looked up and summoned a wave of sand, sending her back even farther across the room and even farther from the door.

Diana jumped back up onto her feet. No longer on the defense. She was ready for a fight.

"Oh, how feisty," Tario taunted. "That won't be enough; I'm through playing around with you and humoring Zane on this ludicrous situation."

"Zane is only doing what my father asked him to do."

"Your father is a weak fool," Tario snapped. "And it doesn't really matter what he thinks anymore, does it? With Warrick gone, Malvin can bring Sabnare into a new era."

"Malvin is a traitor! He is working with the soothsayer."

"Traitor?" Tario laughed, "And what would you know of it? Sabnare is not your home; you have no claim to this place, and you certainly don't know what's best for it," he scoffed.

Tario looked at her with disgust. It was apparent how very little he thought of her, and the feeling was mutual. Diana felt a rage and a hurt building like she had never experienced before.

"I'm going to do everything I can to stop the soothsayer. Whether you think I can or not."

"Arrogance doesn't suit you. Malvin has everything under control," Tario said. "And even if there was any doubt. Zane could handle anything that arises without your interference."

"For someone who thinks so highly of Zane, it's surprising you'd betray his trust like this."

Tario aggressively gestured across his body, causing a wall of sand to collide with Diana. Diana crashed into a shelf, sending it and dream shards flying.

"Don't you dare speak of him!" Tario's face went red. His chest heaved, and a vein began pulsating out of his neck. "Everything I do, I do for him."

As she got up from the rubble, she looked at the mess of a man in front of her. Then it hit her.

"You're in love with him, aren't you?"

Tario refused to look her in the eye.

"That's why you did it, you want him to be a hero," she said, beginning to put the pieces together.

Tario looked up. Angry and exposed, his face contorted into a scowl.

"For some reason, Zane and Warrick think you are some kind of savior," he spat. "I tried to reason with him. I told him that there was no reason for him to bring you here. That he was capable enough on his own to take on anything that could arise." Tario's whole body shook with rage as he stalked towards Diana. "But would he listen to me, his oldest friend, his most trusted confidant? No. He decided that the saving hope of Sabnare rested in the hands of someone who had never even set foot here. It's such a huge disgrace."

The hair on Diana's arms stood on end. Tario's eyes bulged, and she could sense a frantic energy radiating from him. Diana stole glances around the room, trying to figure a way out without giving anything away to Tario.

Out of the corner of his eye, Tario noticed Diana's scroll lying on the floor.

"What's this we have here?" He asked, reaching for it.

"That's mine!"

"And just what are you going to do about it?"

Diana leapt for the scroll. Tario shifted the sand. It formed around Diana's wrists, holding her in place. She struggled against the sand, but his shift was holding strong. He continued for the scroll. Just as his finger reached the scroll, a huge burst of energy zapped him away. He let out a scream and recoiled in pain.

"I still can't touch it. . . what have you done to it?"

Diana looked confused.

"I haven't done anything with the scroll; I barely know how to use the . . ."

A blurry vision from the sorina wreckage flashed in Diana's mind. Flames jumping and a figure reaching out. Reaching for the scroll.

"You were the one at the wreckage," she said. "Seems like an awfully brave move to stick around. Or did you feel safe because I had already eliminated the threat?"

"Don't you dare mock me!"

Tario made a motion, and the sand pulled Diana's arms in different directions. Diana could feel her muscles straining against his shift. She tried to step backward and break free, but she couldn't get the proper traction in the sand. The force of Tario's pull grew stronger. Diana tried to keep a strong face, but her legs were trembling.

"I think it's time for all this to come to an end," he said.

Tario raised two large pillars of sand. They shifted into a form with the tops looking like mallets. Diana watched as they rose above her into striking position. The sand condensed and became less mutable and more solid. The pillars pulled back, ready to release.

Tario's red face dripped in sweat as he channeled the energy for the shift. His whole body quivered as the energy built up within him. He let out a primal scream as he released the energy, and the sand mallets came slamming down.

The scroll darted into position over Diana. It surrounded itself in a bubble of energy. The mallets slammed into the shield. The scroll fell to the floor as the sand reverted into a loose cloud, raining down around them. Obscuring their vision.

Diana could barely see through the sand settling through the air.

Tario was trying to wipe the sand from his eyes. She pulled against her restraints and easily broke free.

She made a break for a door. The quick movement caught Tario's eye. Sand reached up and snared Diana around the neck and brought her crashing to the ground.

The air was still clouded with sand, making it hard to gather her bearings. She felt herself begin to rise into the air. Hoisted up by her neck. She clawed at the sand wrapped around her neck like a noose. She kicked as her feet began to dangle above the ground.

The sand began to settle. Diana could see Tario standing in front of her.

"This is where it ends for you," he said coldly.

Diana looked at him and then looked behind him at the door. So close, yet so out of reach. Tario reached out his hand and began to squeeze. She could feel the sand constricting around her neck. Her breathing became more erratic. With every breath out, the sand grew tighter. Lungs on fire. Eyes welled with tears. She gasped and struggled to break free. The room was fading from view. Diana could feel the end. She felt herself slipping away. She struggled for one last breath.

"Compesco!" a voice bellowed.

Diana dropped to the floor. She reached for her throat to find it clear. She wheezed as she tried to catch her breath. She wiped the tears from her eyes so she could see.

There stood Zane, holding the genie bottle that had spilled out of her bag. The bottle was glowing, and the stopper shot off the top. The stopper separated into two rocky bangles and slid over Tario's wrist. Tario fought to pull them off, but it was no use. Tario's face was filled with betrayal as he looked at Zane standing stoic, bottle in hand. Tario's face filled with tears as his body began turning into pink smoke. It worked its way up his legs, then engulfed the rest of his body as he began to be pulled inside the bottle. Tario's arms flew above his head, and his face was the last bit to fade into smoke, swirling into the bottle. As the last bit of smoke entered the bottle, the wrist bangles reformed into the bottle's stopper. Sealing Tario into the bottle.

"I'm sorry, my friend," Zane said, staring at the bottle in his hand. He looked up at Diana. "Are you okay?"

"I'm not sure if okay is the word," Diana replied, "but I'm still here."

Diana stood up, dusting herself off. Her body was sore. Her neck was red and tender from the abrasive sand, which matched the markings around her wrists.

"I thought I could trust him," Zane said. "I knew he was loyal to Malvin, but I never thought he'd betray me like this."

"He wanted you to be the one to save Sabnare. He didn't think I had any business being here. That's why he lured the slumbra to the oasis to eliminate me."

"Tario always did hold me on a pedestal. Ever since we were young, fledgling sandmen, we did everything together. We worked. We trained. Together, we made our way up the ranks. Eventually, we each caught the eye of a different mentor."

"Warrick and Malvin."

"Correct. Warrick and Malvin took an interest in us. I went under the tutelage of Warrick, and Tario went under Malvin's. Tario wanted us to be together, but that wasn't how it worked. For the first time, we weren't inseparable. We'd be away from each other sometimes, days at a time, depending on our tasks. When we would get back, we'd spend the evenings discussing what we've learned."

"So, you began to drift apart?" Diana asked.

"The answer is more complicated than a yes or a no. We were still close, but Malvin's influence over Tario became stronger and more apparent as time went on. Malvin is very particular about how things should be and doesn't allow much room for interpretation or variance. Warrick's style, however, is much more laid back. He allows for you to make the lessons your own."

"So, Tario didn't like that you weren't doing things in the way that Malvin did them?"

"That is part of it. I also believe he longed for the freedom I had but didn't know how to express it. His loyalty to both Malvin and myself blinded him to other possibilities. He has a good heart but has been led to believe there are very black-and-white rules of how things are done."

Zane looked at the bottle again and sighed. "Well, let's head back to Warrick's quarters, and I will fill you and Yume in on what I discovered."

Zane reached out his hand to Diana's and led her to the door. The scroll flew between them, showing the layout of the castle.

"Looks like it's all clear," she said.

They made their way down the hallways and the twists and turns of the castle. The glowing crystals leading their way.

"I made it down to the dungeons. Delfina has some sandman standing guard, so I couldn't get in to see what is happening inside to the sandmen and baku she's holding captive. I believe the guards may be under some kind of spell."

Diana and Zane came to the entrance to the courtyard. They checked the scroll to be sure they were clear to cross and slipped into Warrick's chamber.

Yume was in the middle of a sea of scrolls and parchment. Zane closed the door. The sound spooked Yume and sent her spiraling up in the air so she could see what the noise was.

"You're back!" she said, settling back to the ground. "You'll never guess what I found."

Yume shuffled through the paper with her trunk and pulled out a small leather journal. She hopped over to them and set the book on an open table. She flipped it open to a page marked with a ribbon.

"Here it is," Yume said. She pointed to a passage with her trunk and began to read aloud. "I never thought it would come to this. I never believed that Delfina had that kind of potential for evil. I know what I must do. After many years of preparing, I hope I can prevent the foreseen events from unfolding." Yume looked up at Zane and Diana. "And that's where it ends."

Diana reached out for the journal. Rereading the passage to herself over and over. She passed it over to Zane, who was waiting for a better look. She watched as he read. His face gave nothing away about what he was thinking.

"Well, it seems we can confirm that Warrick and Delfina knew each other and that this goes deeper than we thought," Zane said.

"Yeah, it seems he knew about this for much longer than we thought, it's not something that just happened." Diana replied, "Did you find anything else, Yume?"

"I didn't find anything else in any of these other writings," she said. "However, I did find a set of scrolls that appear to be blood-locked. So, it appears you are the only one who can open them. What did you all find out?"

"Well, I think I know what my father was talking about. I was able to use the dream viewer to see what was on the shard. It wasn't super clear, but it showed Delfina, and it looks like she wants to destroy the Diamond of Dreams."

Yume gasped. Zane went pale.

Yume looked at Zane, "Didn't she tell you that already?"

"No, we didn't have time we had a situation that needed to be resolved," he said, hanging his head.

Yume looked from Zane to Diana and back. Waiting for a response. When it was clear that Zane wasn't going to elaborate, Diana spoke up.

"Tario showed up and tried to kill me," she said, "and he would have done it if Zane hadn't stepped in and trapped him in a genie bottle."

Yume's mouth hung open. She looked back at Zane. "Are you alright?"

"I'm fine, I did what I had to do," he cleared his throat, "anyway, what I found out is that Delfina has bewitched sandmen guarding the door to the dungeon. We need to figure out a plan to get past them."

"If only there was a way we could be escorted down there without actually being captured," Yume said.

If only it were that easy. It's not like they could just walk themselves right past the guards. Something was stirring at the back of Diana's mind. *What if we could do just that?*

"Wait a minute, I think I have an idea," she said.

Diana began digging through her pouches. She knew it was in there. She pulled out the spell book from her mother and began to flip through the pages. She could have sworn she had seen a spell that could help. She continued flipping until she was almost at the back of the book.

"Aha, I thought I remembered seeing this."

She showed the page to Zane and Yume. A page containing a spell called Chains of Enchantment.

"How does this help us?" Zane asked.

"It's just like Yume said: we need to be escorted down to the dungeon, but the only way to do so is to be captured. But what if I pose as one of Delfina's bewitched guards? I can lead you down using these chains to look like you've been caught."

Diana smiled. She thought she had come up with a rather clever plan. The looks on her companions' faces told another story. Yume's face was thoughtful as she seemed to be working out the scenario in her head. Zane, however, did not look convinced. Skepticism was scrawled all over his normal, nonreactive face. Diana could see that she would really have to sell the idea. Yume was the first to speak up.

"I think it could work," she said reassuringly.

"What do you think Zane?" Diana asked.

"I think it's very risky," he said, "I should be the one to lead us down."

"That would be well and good if you were the one who could conjure the chains. It has to be me. Besides, we will need you both to look like you're struggling against the chains to be brought there. It would be hard for me to do that and keep my identity hidden beneath my robes."

Zane's eyebrow raised as he considered what Diana said.

"It can work," she said. Trying to convince Zane.

"I think we should trust her, Zane," Yume said.

"Okay," Zane said with a sigh, "let's give it a try."

EIGHTEEN

Diana crept down the hall with her friends in tow. Magical chains bound them to her as she followed the scroll's directions to the dungeon. Diana was wrapped up in her robes. Concealing her identity.

They went lower and lower into the bowels of the castle. As large as the castle was from above, it seemed to be just as large underground. Its size was incomprehensible, let alone how anyone could navigate it on their own. As they traveled down, the corridors became cold and damp, sending a chill down Diana.

They arrived at the bottom of a dingy stairwell. The scroll floated in place in front of them, its wings flapping, waiting.

"It's just down the hallway from here," said Zane.

Diana took a deep breath. She readjusted her robes, tucking away her ponytail, making sure they wouldn't be able to see who she was. "Alright, I think I'm ready how about you guys?"

"I'm ready," Yume said, her normal chipper tone nowhere to be heard.

"Ready," said Zane.

Diana reached for the scroll and tucked it away into her robes.

"Here we go," she said, "just like we practiced."

Diana stepped out into the hallway, dragging her friends in tow. Zane and Yume struggled against the chains as they walked. Diana continued forward, head down as they approached the door. The bewitched sandmen stood there standing guard, their faces blank and eyes dull.

"C'mon," she said in her gruffest voice, pulling the chains. Zane pretended to stumble as the chains pulled against his bound wrists. Yume dug in her feet as she was being dragged across the floor. She then flew up and floated back down, feigning weakness. Diana was very impressed by their performance.

They approached the guards.

"Let us through," Diana said in a gruff voice, "We've got some new volunteers."

The guards looked over the group. Yume stood there shaking, looking terrified. Zane was hunched over, breathing heavily. They both were dirty, covered in sweat and sand.

"Good, Delfina will be pleased," said the first guard.

"Make sure you secure them well," said the second guard, "she won't tolerate any more mistakes.

The guards pushed open the door and stepped aside. Diana dragged her companions forward. They headed down the stairs. There was a thud as the door was shut behind them. They continued down the stairs, where they came to a final door. Diana pulled on it. The door wouldn't budge. She tried again with no luck.

"It's locked," she said.

"Oh no," Yume said, "what should we do?"

"Try your key," Zane suggested.

Diana reached into her robes. Rummaging around in her pouch and pockets, her finger grazed across the key. She took the key and placed it in the keyhole. Diana took a deep breath. With firm resolve, she gave the key a twist. There was a clang as the lock released, and the door opened into the room.

They stepped into the dank room. Diana dismissed the chains

with a motion of her hands. Zane rubbed his wrists, and Yume twisted her neck, relieving their stiff muscles.

Diana pulled out the scroll. It fluttered to life and displayed the floor plan of the dungeon. The main room was large and lined with doors leading to holding cells. At the far end of the room was another hallway. Looking at the scroll, Diana could see the dungeon coiled around like a snake, leaving a wide, empty space in the castle's center.

"This place is huge," Diana said, taking it all in.

"Look there at the end of the tunnel," Zane said, pointing to the map. "Those dots are people, right? So, I think that's where we need to head."

"Sounds like a plan to me," said Yume.

"Alright, let's keep moving," Diana said. "We don't want the guards to wonder what's taking so long."

They headed down into the spiraling dungeon tunnel. Diana's scroll floated in front of them, leading the way. Like the rest of the hallways of the castle, they were lined with glowing purple crystals. These, however, were much dimmer and flickered weakly, making their shadows dance eerily across the walls.

As they walked, Diana peered into the cells. It was hard to make out, but some cells looked like they were covered in claw marks. Others appeared to have scorch marks where the sand became onyx-colored glass. She could only imagine what these cells had been used for.

The group walked in silence. Not wanting to attract attention. The only sound was the crunch of the damp sand beneath their feet.

Further into the tunnel, they could hear noise coming from the end. With every step, the sounds got louder. It was hard to distinguish what the sounds were. Each step was filled with trepidation. Not knowing what to expect.

They came to the final turn marked on the map. The scroll stopped moving forward. Zane signaled for everyone to get against the wall. They crept to the edge of the wall, where the muffled sound of voices and trumpeting accosted their ears.

Zane peered around the corner. Yume floated above him, hugging the wall, also attempting to see what awaited them.

Zane stepped out into the hallway and entered the room. Diana and Yume followed closely behind him. Diana gasped at the sight before them.

Two sandmen in hoods were bound to large wooden tables. Startled by Diana's gasp, they began fighting against their restraints. Their muffled cries filled the chamber. The noise of the struggling sandmen set off a wave of trumpeting and wails from the very back of the room. The back quarter of the room was fashioned into a large cage with bars running across it. Behind the bars were several baku.

Diana snapped back into focus. "Yume, go check on the other baku while Zane and I attend to the sandmen. Yume darted over towards the cell with a trail of smoke behind her while Diana and Zane each approached a sandman.

Diana removed her sandman's hood. His eyes widened with fear, his screams muffled by the gag in his mouth. Diana gently placed her hand on his arm, trying to calm him down.

"Shhh, it's okay," she said. "We're here to help you."

The sandman continued to struggle and thrash his head about. Screaming against the gag. He kept looking around until his eyes landed on Zane helping the other sandman, who had finally stopped crying out. He looked for a moment, then turned his head back, looking at the ceiling. His eyes filled with tears of relief as his whole body quivered.

Diana rubbed his arm. "It's okay," she said, "It's all over now."

The tears ran down his face as Diana undid the gag. Diana looked over the restraints, trying to figure out how to undo them. He lay there with his ankles bound next to each other by metal brackets. Moving upwards, there was another metal restraint over his waist. His torso was exposed, and another piece of metal went over his neck to hold his head and wrists in place.

Diana looked over the shackles. She wasn't sure how to release them. She looked for a keyhole or anything that could undo them. She came up empty. Diana remembered how Zane had opened the door to Warrick's without a keyhole. She retrieved her key, pointed it towards the binding, and focused her intention. She gave the key a turn. Nothing. The sandman remained locked to the table. At the other table, it appeared that Zane was having similar issues.

"We will figure this out," she said, "while we are looking for a solution, can you tell me what happened?"

The sandman continued to stare at the ceiling. "I'm not sure how it happened. We were in the village when a bunch of sandmen moon-beamed in. They said they were at the oasis and that the sorina had been attacked and destroyed by a slumbra. Once the survivors were settled, the two of us moon-beamed out to the oasis to see what we could find and what could be salvaged. Trees were smashed, and there were these large glass-like structures streaked across the sand. We didn't see the sorina anywhere."

"Then what happened?"

"We came across some ostrock tracks. We began to follow them to see which way they went. Then we were ambushed."

"By who?"

"The dreamons," he said. "Before we knew it, they were rising from the sand. We were surrounded. We tried to fight them off, but there were too many. They drained us of our energy so we could no longer use our powers and dragged us to the castle. That's when she arrived. She flew down as an owl and transformed into a woman. She seemed to be controlling the dreamon. It was hard to tell what was happening. Then they brought us down here where we've been waiting."

"Do you know what it is that she wants?"

"No," he said and struggled against the shackles, "have you figured out how to release us yet?"

"Not yet, but I'm going to go talk with my friends and figure it out."

Diana stepped away from the sandman. She made a motion for Zane to join her. He stepped away from his sandman and reconvened with Diana.

"Any idea on how to get them off the tables?" she asked, hopefully.

"I'm not sure. I don't know how they were summoned. This isn't a sandman's magic. I think we need a witch to undo it. So that means it's up to you to release them."

"But I have no idea how to do that," she said.

Before she could say another word, Yume rejoined them. She looked pale.

"What did you find out, Yume?" Zane asked.

The fear on Yume's face couldn't be hidden. Her eyes to the brim with tears.

"I can hardly believe what they told me. It seems that the soothsayer found a way to drain baku of their power." She paused; tears streaked down her face. "Benjiro, he. . . he fought as hard as he could. She drained his power until he couldn't hold out anymore."

"What reason could she have for wanting to absorb bakus' power?" Zane asked.

"She's using the dream-eating ability to steal the powers of sandmen. Sandmen are made of dream sand, so she is absorbing them in hopes of acquiring their powers."

"Do you think that's what happened to my dad?" Diana asked. Panic and a million different scenarios ran through her mind. *Could it already be too late?*

"I don't think so. Warrick seemed to be a step ahead." Zane said.

Diana relaxed a little, not completely convinced. She needed more answers.

"Yume, did they say what she wants the powers for?" Diana asked.

"No, none of them have any idea," Yume replied.

"If that's the case, we had better hurry I don't think she'd want to leave them down here too long," Zane said. "Diana, is there a spell in your book that could help?"

"None that I know off the top of my head," she replied. "Let me flip through really quick."

Diana pulled out the spell book and flipped through the pages. Hoping something would jump out at her. As she flipped, a page caught her eye as it passed. She turned back to the page. It was an unbinding spell. It said:

If you feel that your magic is bound. Cast this spell; it won't take a sound. With a wave of the hand, all will be grand.

Diana looked at the diagram. She mimicked the movements that were written in front of her. It's worth a shot, she thought to herself.

"I found something. I'm not sure if it's right, but I'm going to try it."

Diana walked over to the sandman she had been trying to help. "Hey there, I'm going to try something to get you out of this, okay? So just stay calm, and hopefully, this will work as planned."

Diana took a step back. She took a deep breath in and released it slowly, helping her to ground and center. She focused on what she wanted to happen. She could see it in her mind as the last bit of breath was ready to escape. She did the motions from the book. Finishing with the last of her breath. The shackles glowed orange momentarily and went out. She tried again. The same thing happened. Glowing, but no release.

"I'm not sure what's happening," she said.

"If that and your key didn't work," Zane said. "We will have to try something else."

An idea popped into Diana's head, and a smile spread across her face.

"What is it?" Yume asked.

"Zane's right I need to use my key," she said.

"What do you mean?" he asked, bewildered. "How can you use the key; there's no keyhole, and it didn't work before?"

"I have an idea," she said, "trust me."

Diana changed positions. She was standing evenly between the two tables. She held the key in her hand. With her eyes closed, she took in a deep breath and focused on what she wanted. She let the breath out. She took another deep breath, focusing on the moves of the spell. As she began to exhale, she began doing the moves. She held the key in her hand like a wand and focused all her energy through the key until it began to glow orange.

Diana recreated the movements of the spell, tracing the pattern through the air with her key. An orange aura that matched the key began to radiate from the shackles that held the sandmen. On the final flick, the glowing of the key and restraints came to a crescendo. The light faded away along with the shackles, and the sandmen were no longer prisoners to the table.

Diana and Zane ran over to the sandmen, helping them down off the table. Diana was relieved that her plan worked, but there was no time to celebrate.

A large commotion came from the cage holding the baku. The sight of the freed sandmen was too much for the baku to contain their emotions. The herd was trumpeting and squealing like animals being led to slaughter. Yume tried calming them down, but the herd was so lost in their emotions they didn't even hear her. Diana scurried over to the cage to assist Yume.

"Everyone, please be quiet, we don't want anyone to come to check things out," Diana pleaded.

Her pleas fell on deaf ears. The herd didn't calm down. Their frenzy only increased in intensity. Baku with large tusks rammed at the bars. Others flew up to the ceiling, trying to break free. Zane approached the bars, trying to calm the herd.

Yume looked back and forth between her friends and at the panicking baku. She closed her eyes. Sparkling pink smoke began to pour out from her wrists and ankles. Her eyes opened to reveal a bright purple light. She let out a mighty trumpet from her trunk. The smoke began to swirl around her body, encompassing it like a raging storm. Most of the baku were still rampaging in the cell. However, several baku that were in the front of the cell began to settle, watching the scene unfold. The smoke swirled, flashed, and expanded.

Diana and Zane grabbed the other sandmen and took a few steps back. The baku, who were all now at attention, followed suit. With a large gust, the smoke dissipated to every corner of the dungeon. Revealing Yume. At least, they thought it was Yume.

Standing there was a much larger baku. Yume's body had grown muscular and leaner, like that of a tiger. She now sported longer, slender ears and modest tusks. A mane of smoke billowed around her neck. It matched her new smokey tail and cuffs around her ankles, which now led to impressive claws. She let out a deafening trumpet that reverberated through Diana's body. Yume charged into the cage door. She hooked her tusk around one of the bars and dug her claws into the sandy floor for traction. The glowing of her eyes intensified as her tusks began to glow as well. Yume struggled against the bars, and then, with one sharp move, her tusk ripped through the bars, and they exploded into sand. A victorious trumpet erupted from Yume's trunk. No one moved.

The glow in her eyes subsided. Yume lurched to the ground. A wave of smoke washed over her body, revealing her regular body as the smoke cleared.

"Yume!" Diana called out as she and Zane rushed to their friend's side. The baku in the cell apprehensively stepped forward and surrounded the group.

Yume looked up through partially opened eyes, "Is everything okay?"

"It sure is, you were phenomenal," Zane said.

"Not to sound insensitive," chimed in one of the sandmen, "but can we get going?"

Zane looked at Diana, "He's right we don't have the luxury of time."

"Yeah, we've already spent more time down here than we should have." Diana agreed. "Yume, are you okay to get going?"

Yume struggled to get to her feet. She took a few shaky steps forward.

"We will help her."

A yellow and blue male baku with a sparkling blue mane stepped forward. He bent down, scooping Yume up in his large tusks.

"Thank you," Diana said before turning back to Zane. "So, what's the plan for dealing with the guards when we reach the top?"

"Just leave that to me," Zane said.

NINETEEN

Zane led the way through the dimly lit, spiraling underground of the castle's dungeon with the aid of Diana's scroll. She followed behind him with the rescued sandmen. Diana looked behind her to the baku holding Yume in his tusks.

"Are you still doing alright with her?" she asked.

"I am fine, thank you," he replied, giving a slight bow of his head.

"I'm sorry in all of the commotion, I didn't get your name," Diana said.

"It's Takeshi," he replied.

"Pleasure to meet you."

The group continued rising out of the bowels of the castle. The only sound was from their footsteps and the scroll's fluttering wings as they trudged through the twisting dungeon. Making their way towards the exit. Zane came to a stop at the first door.

"Okay, everyone, just like we talked about," Zane said, "Diana if you'd unlock the door."

Diana stepped forward to use her key. Turning it with care to not make too much noise with the latch. Zane continued leading the group. Each step of the final stairwell felt like an eternity. At the top, he checked the scroll and cracked open the door. He saw one of the guards. Just beyond the guard, a long empty hallway.

Zane raised his hand. Slowly, the sand in the hallway began to flow. Another motion of his hand and the movement picked up. Zane began making a circular motion with his finger. The sand began to swirl and rise, filling the hallway like a snow globe. The guards took a few steps towards the shifting sand to investigate. With another sharp movement of his hand, Zane whipped up the sand into a frenzy. The guards covered their faces with their arms. The visibility was poor as the sand flew in every direction.

Zane busted into the hallway, kicking open the door. His hands focused on the raging sandstorm.

"Run!" he yelled.

The guards turned to see what was happening. Zane began to run to the next stairwell with the prisoners in tow. The guards raised their hands, preparing to shift.

"Catena ligare!" Diana shouted while pointing her wand at the guards. Glowing chains shot up from the ground. The cuffs locked on their wrists with a clank, impeding their ability to shift the sand. Diana followed the stampeding herd of baku and sandmen.

Diana was unable to focus on her surroundings as she ran. The scroll flew in front of her. The glowing crystals that lit the way streaked past like cars on the highway. The sound of the guard's voices echoed behind her. She knew, when she cast the spell, that her chains wouldn't hold long. Now, the guards were in pursuit.

The baku and sandmen poured out of the castle as the stairwell opened to the courtyard. The group stopped and began to gather in the center, allowing Diana to catch up from the rear.

A movement of darkness caught Diana's eye. Dreamons were beginning to materialize, clawing at the air while rising out of the ground. The shadowy creatures surrounded the group, reaching out with their long, slender fingers.

Zane thrust a hand down to the ground. The sand sprung to life with his shift, spinning around them to create a wall of protection. The dreamon repositioned themselves, moving like schooling fish around the barrier, trying to break through.

"This won't hold them back for long," Zane said. "We are going to have to fight our way out."

"Dream shield," Diana yelled, raising her arm and summoning her dream catcher shield. "Zane, look out!"

A dreamon began to appear, crawling up from the sand inside the barrier. Its shadowy hand latched onto Zane's ankle, pulling him to the ground. As Zane hit the ground, the barrier fell with him.

The dreamon started closing in. The sandmen, still weak from capture, shifted waves of sand at the dreamon. The dreamon remained mostly unphased. It was more of an annoyance than a hindrance.

"Devour the dreamon!" Takeshi shouted. Yume began to wake at the sound of Takeshi's voice, and he placed her down gently.

The baku charged. From the sky and ground, they attacked. Smoke against shadow. A red and orange baku hovered above a dreamon. Its smoke billowed, and its eyes released a stunning amber glow as it began to vacuum up the dreamon with its trunk.

Zane struggled on the ground. The dreamon still had hold of him, making him weak. Takeshi threw back his head and let out an intimidating trumpet. His tusks glistened in the light of Sabnare's moons. He charged towards Zane, knocking dreamon out of the way with his tusks.

Takeshi's eyes lit up, blue sparkling smoke pouring from his mane as he began to absorb the dreamon. Desperate to cling to anything, the dreamon reached out as his body was sucked away until nothing was left. Takeshi blew out a strong puff of smoke as the dreamon was devoured. Reaching down with his trunk, he helped Zane to his feet before taking off towards another dreamon.

Diana stared into the featureless face of a dreamon. Its glowing eyes pulsed as it rushed towards her. Diana raised her shield as its arm slammed down on the shield. A bright light blasted from the shield, disintegrating the arm. The dreamon released an unearthly howl while it turned and fled.

"Stop!" she called, reaching out her hand. A ball of fire launched from her palm. The fire engulfed the dreamon, and it disappeared.

Diana held out her hand, trying to bring on another fireball. The fire flickered in her hand like a faulty lighter. Finally, she was able to conjure another. She promptly launched it at another dreamon. Obliterating it on contact.

Yume flew overhead. "We need to clear a path so that everyone can escape."

Diana looked over and saw the gateway that led back into the Desert of Dreams. That's where the highest concentration of dreamon were. She ran towards the cluster. Diana focused her energy. Heat spread through her body and concentrated in her hands. She shoved out her arms, releasing a flame thrower of varying intensity. The dreamons backed away, clearing a path. She let off a few more blasts. The flames consumed several dreamon, and others began to recede into the sand.

"Everybody run!" Diana commanded. "We'll keep them occupied."

The rescued sandmen and baku made a break for the outside. Baku stampeded on the ground and through the air. At the same time, the sandmen sand-surfed out into the Desert of Dreams. The last of the dreamon left the courtyard, retreating into the sand as the others made their escape.

"What now?" Yume asked, landing next to Diana and Zane.

The sound of an owl's screech came from above before anyone could answer. The owl had burst from a window in one of the towers. Diving down towards the courtyard like a missile. Pulling up as it dived and banked to the side. It landed and began to ripple and change. Its feathers faded from view, replaced by a tattered cloak, as the figure grew into the soothsayer.

"I wish the exits were sealed!" the soothsayer yelled, holding out a genie's bottle.

The top of the bottle popped out, hovering above the bottle. A cloud of smoke exited the bottle and swirled around the courtyard. As the smoke passed over, the exits were replaced with solid walls. Trapping everyone within. The smoke made its way next to the soothsayer. The bottle's top floated over the smoke as it began to change and take form.

The stopper split into two bangles. Tendrils of smoke reached up, passing through the rocky wristlets as the smoke began to corporealize. Hands formed through the top of the bangles, followed by arms. The smoke rippled down like water, revealing a figure who now stood before them.

The genie's smooth, dark skin glowed like the new moon. Her long white dreads swayed down to the small of her back. Her eyes were a familiar purple.

Zane's mouth fell open. "Ada?"

She averted her eyes from his, her body rigid.

"Oh, so you know each other," Delfina chortled, "she has been very useful in granting me access to Sabnare."

Zane's brow furled as he clenched his teeth, and his fists shook at his sides. His eyes darted between Ada and Delfina. He looked like a bull about to charge. Sand began to swirl at his feet as he glared at the soothsayer.

"How dare you!"

Zane took a step towards Delfina.

"Back!" she yelled, thrusting out Ada's bottle.

Ada's eyes glowed, and a blast sent Zane, Diana, and Yume flying across the courtyard.

Diana and Zane struggled back to their feet as Ada hung her head. Diana looked for Yume and found her. Knocked out, laying on the other side of the yard.

"Yume!" she cried out. She turned to Delfina, "Why are you doing this?"

Delfina's eyes narrowed. "I will regain what is rightfully mine, and no one is going to stand between me and my dreams anymore."

"You have no power here," Zane snarled.

Delfina smirked, stepping purposefully towards Zane. "You have no idea about the measure of my power. Even as you try to keep it subdued."

Delfina reached out her hand. In a flash, a sword appeared, summoned to her grasp. She raised the sword above her head, preparing to strike. The sword came slamming down towards Zane.

As the sword struck, the sound of shattering glass filled the air. Diana screamed. Tario's bottle had leapt from her side, intercepting Delfina's deadly blow.

Tario's shattered bottle lay in pieces in front of Zane. The pieces glowed faintly as pink smoke rose from the debris. Tario's smokey silhouette took shape, staring at Zane, eyes full of tears."

"I'm sorry," Tario wept, "I'm sorry for everything. I wanted you to be the one to take care of everything. I didn't think you needed any help defending Sabnare." He looked briefly at Diana before returning to Zane. "I felt Warrick didn't believe enough in you," he paused, "as much as I do. I love you."

He reached out for Zane. The bottle stopped glowing. Its pieces reverted to sand as Tario's smokey form dissolved, leaving no trace as his remains rejoined the sand of the courtyard. Zane grabbed a fist full of sand where the bottle pieces had been. He looked up at Delfina. A tear ran down his cheek just as the sand ran through his fingers.

"Zane," Diana said, "you're bleeding."

A trail of blood rolled down Zane's arm from a gash left by Delfina's sword. The blood dripped into the sand, pooling where Tario's shattered bottle had been.

Delfina laughed. "That's what happens when you get in my way."

Diana thrust her arms forward. A wall of sand collided with Delfina, shoving her across the ground. Delfina tumbled to her feet as her summoned sword disappeared.

Diana took a moment to evaluate Zane's injury. The gash was deep. She ripped a piece from her robes and tied it around his arm.

Delfina rose to her feet. A scowl etched across her face. Her body was rigid.

"So, Warrick thinks that you can defeat me." She said, raising an arm, preparing to conjure. "I will destroy both of you and anyone who dares to get in my way!"

A blur of pink and purple slammed into her side. Delfina looked down to see Yume running towards Diana, and she had the genie bottle wrapped in her trunk. Delfina's eyes widened with rage.

Yume ran over to Diana, handing her the bottle. Diana took the bottle and smiled. She had an idea. She placed her hands on Zane and Yume. Leaning in, she whispered into the bottle so the soothsayer couldn't hear. "I wish we were safely back in the village."

In a sudden swirl of smoke, they were gone. Leaving the castle and Delfina behind.

CHAPTER
TWENTY

The swirling smoke cloud cleared, revealing the interior of Warrick's home in the village. Diana sat Zane down on the couch and retrieved the spell book from the pouch at her side.

"Is he going to be alright?" Yume asked.

"He sure will, once I look up the healing spell," Diana said. She noticed cuts along Yume's side. "Yume, why don't you hop up there next to Zane? That way, I can tend to you as well."

Yume curled up at Zane's side, leaving her wounds exposed. Diana looked at her injured friends. Yume, despite being hurt, was still basically her jubilant self. Zane, however, was a different story. He seemed much more withdrawn than usual. His eyes not looking up from the floor. Arms crossed; one hand held his wound.

Diana reread the spell and then put the book away. She held out her wand, its tip glowing with healing energy. She let the energy pulsate and flow from its tip. Energy rippled down on her friends. Their wounds began to glow a greenish-blue, growing smaller as they healed. The light from the wand went out as the last of the energy settled in. It was as if the wounds had never been there.

Diana removed the bandage from Zane's arm. "There, all better." Zane didn't say a word or look up. "Why don't you lay down for a bit?"

Yume hopped off the couch and placed a pillow in her place. Diana guided Zane down. If only the spell could have healed his spirit as well as his body. As he placed his head on the pillow, his eyes focused on something behind Diana. He looked for a moment, then closed his eyes.

Diana and Yume turned to see what he had been staring at. There in the corner stood Ada, quietly observing. Diana let out a small gasp in surprise.

"I'm sorry, I did not mean to startle you," Ada said.

Diana collected herself. "No, you're fine, thank you for getting us out of there."

"It was your wish that did," she replied. "I merely facilitated."

"Well, either way, thank you. I'm Diana," she said, taking a step forward and reaching out her hand.

"Ada," she replied with a slight nod, stepping forward to return the gesture.

"And I'm Yume."

Ada nodded at the baku.

"Would you join us for some tea?" Diana asked, motioning to the kitchen.

Diana began to prepare the tea. Ada and Yume made themselves comfortable around the small table. Diana served the tea. Yume's mug had a special handle. It was designed to make it easier for her trunk to hold. Ada took the mug Diana handed her. The image on its side caught her off guard. It featured a black and purple dragon on it surrounded by little purple stones.

"Is everything okay?" Diana asked, sipping from the cow mug in her hands.

"Oh yes," Ada said, snapping out of it, "everything is fine."

Ada smiled, taking a sip from the mug. Its floral scent lingered in the air. It had been a long time since she'd had the simple comfort of tea.

Diana looked past Ada towards the back of the couch. Ada followed her gaze.

"Zane is strong," Ada reassured her, "he will be alright."

"Ada's right," Yume said, "nothing to worry about."

Diana sipped her tea. She knew deep down they were right. However, it did very little to ease her worry.

"So, how do you know Zane?" Diana asked.

"We have known each other since we were much younger," Ada replied.

"Why did he seem so surprised to see you?" Diana asked.

Ada looked over at the couch. "We were very close back then." She turned back to Diana. "I have not been present in Sabnare in a very long time. I left with no warning, through no choice of my own. I would guess he never really knew what happened."

"Why did you have to leave so suddenly?" Yume asked sweetly.

"A genie is one who has choices made for them in an effort to manifest others desires."

A silence rolled over the table like a dense fog. Each of them sipped their tea. Diana and Yume stole glances at each other. Neither of them knew what to say. Ada continued to drink her tea, avoiding eye contact.

"I apologize," Ada said, "I did not mean to make the conversation uncomfortable."

"No, I'm sorry," Diana said, "it seems like you have been through a lot."

"I'm sure your encounter with the soothsayer didn't help either," added Yume.

"You are correct," Ada said, "the soothsayer needed access to Sabnare. Sabnare is protected from outsiders so as to not offset the balance of things. Only those of Sabnare can travel freely between the realms to the land of dreams. A sandman would sacrifice themselves before bringing an outsider to Sabnare. Being a genie, I have the ability to cross between the worlds." She paused, "but without the luxury of refusing admittance."

"I wonder why she is doing this," Diana said.

"Too bad you didn't get a chance to read through those locked scrolls we found," Yume said, "maybe the answers are in there."

"Yeah, I wish I had them here," Diana said.

Ada's eyes began to glow. She held out her arms. Smoke began to swirl over her arms. The smoke cleared, revealing the set of scrolls. Ada's eyes returned to normal.

"I believe these are what you wanted," Ada said.

"Oh my god, yes," Diana replied.

Diana reached out and grabbed a few scrolls, placing them on the table. Once Diana had set down most of the scrolls, Ada readjusted the last scroll. She handed it over to Diana. As she did, Ada's finger brushed against the jewel on the scroll. The jewel flashed, and the scroll opened to the floor.

Diana and Yume stood there speechless. Eyes wide, mouths agape. Neither could move. Diana shifted her focus to Ada, her mind racing, trying to process what she had just seen.

"I am so sorry," Ada said as she hurriedly bent over to retrieve the end of the scroll. "It was not my intent to open it."

Ada placed the open scroll on the table. She worked to roll it back up. Diana took her hand into hers.

"I don't think you understand," Diana said, "there is no way you should be able to open them. Warrick sealed them with blood magic." Diana looked into Ada's eyes. They were the same purple as hers. The same as Warrick's. Tears welled up in her eyes until a single tear slid down her face. "I think this means that we are family, that we . . ."

"Sisters . . ." Yume said softly, looking back and forth between them. "How exciting," Yume let out a happy trumpet, floating up from her chair in a cloud of sparkly pink smoke.

Ada retracted her hands, cupping her hands over her heart. Her mouth moved, but no words came out.

Diana smiled cheek to cheek as she wiped away her tears. "It's okay," she said. "You don't have to say anything." She turned to the scrolls. "Let's have a read, shall we?"

Ada nodded and turned to the table. They all looked over the scrolls. Diana read passage after passage and discovered these scrolls told the history of Warrick and Delfina.

"It seems like Warrick and Delfina knew each other quite deeply," Diana said.

"Look what I found here," Ada said. "It talks about how he went dream diving and intercepted a prophetic dream meant for Delfina. It says the vision showed destruction and upheaval. It also says he stashed away the dream shard for further reference. If we can find it, maybe it can reveal some answers."

"I found the dream shard when we were at the castle," Diana said.

"That is wonderful news," Ada replied, "maybe we can access it and see the dream."

"Well, about that," Diana said, avoiding Ada's eyes. "It kind of broke into pieces. So, when I went to access it, well, it wasn't super clear."

In the most diplomatic tone she could muster, Ada replied. "Well, perhaps we can piece it together from what you saw and what was written."

"Hey, you guys, look at this," Yume said, pointing at a section in the scroll she was reading. "Warrick wrote this:

It is clear now from the vision I got and the subsequent visions thereafter that it is my daughter who will be the one who can stop Delfina. The darkness in her is more than I had ever guessed. I must do my

*best to stop it from ever getting to that point. I don't
want my child to have to deal with such darkness."*

"Does it say anything else?" Diana asked.

"No, that's where it ends," said Yume.

"I wonder what steps he took trying to prevent this from happening?" Ada asked.

"Yume, does it say?" Diana asked.

"No, that was the end of that scroll."

Diana tried to make sense of everything she had just learned. Ada also seemed lost in thought while Yume continued to look over the scrolls.

"Seems like we have a bigger piece of the puzzle," Zane said from the doorway.

"Zane!" Chirped Yume.

"How are you feeling?" Diana asked.

"My body is healed," he paused, "for now that will have to do." He turned to Ada. "Ada, it has been so long, my heart is lighter knowing that you are alright." He walked over and embraced Ada. Ada returned the embrace. They held the moment until it parted naturally.

"It is good to see you too, Zane," she said. Her smile was warm and comforting.

"So," Zane said, "we need to decide on our next course of action."

"I think one thing is clear," Diana said, "we can't do this alone. We are going to need as many people as possible."

"I agree," said Ada. "Delfina's power is only growing, and everyone is in danger. We are going to need as many sandmen as possible."

"And baku," Yume said. "We will need members of the herd to help protect Sabnare."

"I agree," Zane said, "only combined do we have enough of a chance to defeat the soothsayer."

"So, it looks like we need to gather everyone," Diana said, "and we need to do it quickly. Delfina is going to be preparing now that she knows we are here."

"Also, with Malvin at her side," Zane said, "we need to get to the sandmen before he does. We can't let anymore fall under their control."

"Where and how should we gather everyone?" Yume asked.

"I think I know just how we should do it," Diana said as a sly grin crept across her face.

TWENTY-ONE

Marching past the pond on the outskirts of the village, the academy appeared before them. Zane smiled as they stopped at the massive wooden doors.

"The academy is a great idea," he said, "we can fit everyone from the village inside."

"Yes, a most appropriate choice," Ada agreed.

They made their way inside the double doors. Zane led the way, following the different paths and stairways. Making their way into the middle of the arena, they scanned the arena.

"Whoa," Yume said, bobbing about in the air, her eyes wide. The grandeur and massive scale of the academy under the eternal night sky of Sabnare was awe-inspiring.

"This will be perfect," Diana said, looking up at the stands proudly.

"Who's there?" a voice called out from the opposite entrance to the arena.

The group turned to look. A large silhouette rapidly approached them. Stepping out of the shadows, a sandman appeared, riding a brilliant white ostrock.

"Raza!" Diana shouted joyfully, smiling from ear to ear.

Raza rode over to the group. "Well, look who we have here," he chuckled. "I wasn't sure you made it after the slumbra attack."

"We could say the same to you, my friend," Zane said.

"What are you doing here?" Raza asked.

"We've come to gather every sandman from the village," Diana said.

"Things are worse than we thought," Zane said, "The soothsayer's reach is greater than we expected. Including being helped by Malvin."

"We have a lot to say and even more to do," Diana said.

"Well, the academy is yours to use," Raza said. "Do you need any assistance in gathering everyone?"

"I do believe that is where I come in," Ada said, stepping forward. "Shall we?"

"Absolutely," Diana said as she held out Ada's bottle, "I wish all the sandmen in the village were here to listen to what we have to say."

Ada's eyes lit up. Her arms were slightly raised at her sides. She began to float into the center of the arena. Her long, beautiful locks swayed as a purple aura emanated from her whole body. She rose, rotating into the air. Her robes and hair were alive in the energy surrounding her. Purple smoke swirled out from her body, covering the stands overlooking the pit. The dense smoke continued to circle the arena. Ada sent out a final pulse of energy before lowering to the ground.

The smoke made a final pass around the stands of the arena. Sandmen now filled the seats that overlooked the arena as the smoke cleared. They looked around, their confused chatter filling the air, echoing off the walls of the arena.

"Attention, friends," Zane shouted, his voice lost in the sea of voices. "Attention!" He cried out to no avail.

"That will never work," Raza said, "let me turn on the amplifier." He rode over to the side wall, near one of the entrances to the arena, where a purple crystal was on the wall. He placed his hand on it and twisted it. A ring of gems circling the pit lit up. The lights extended up the stairs into the stands. The farther he twisted, the farther up the lights went. When they were fully lit, including a ring around the top of the academy, Raza nodded at Zane.

"Attention, friends!" Zane shouted. His voice boomed, shaking the building. Shocked sandmen held their ears. "Sorry, friends," he said in his normal voice, which was now amplified to the perfect level for all to hear. "We have urgent news for you all. The soothsayer has overtaken the castle and is after the Diamond of Dreams."

Murmurs could be heard all over the stadium. Panic and confusion scrawled across their faces as they tried to process such an incomprehensible statement.

"We are going to need everyone's help to retake the castle," Zane continued. "Her power is strong, and if she is able to take control of the Diamond of Dreams, it would be disastrous. Our world as we know it would come to an end."

The crowd's chatter became louder.

"This will not be easy, as she has bewitched many of our own people. And she's not alone in her endeavors. Malvin has been aiding her the whole time."

The crowd erupted. Their angry shouting reverberated throughout the stadium.

"Together, we can take back Sabnare. So that dreams continue to create balance among the realms and keep the worlds running. And so that no one sacrifices that for their own personal agendas."

The crowd cheered.

"This is not the job of sandmen alone; we must reach out to our baku brothers and sisters. Diana and Yume are going to speak with the herd so we can unite as one."

"We will bring all of Sabnare together to save our home!" Yume shouted.

The crowd's cheering grew to a roar.

"As they head off, we will fill you all in on the details of our plan and what we need from each of you to do," Zane instructed.

Zane turned to Diana and Yume.

"Time to head out, Ada, and I will get everything settled here."

"Sounds good we will see you soon," Diana said.

"We've got this under control," Yume chirped.

Diana and Yume made their way across the arena, heading towards the exit.

"Diana, wait!" Ada called out, rushing to catch up. Diana stopped and turned. "Please be careful, and keep my bottle with you in case you need it."

"I will, thank you," Diana said. A shy grin appeared on her face.

"Have no worries," Yume chimed in, "I'll take care of her."

Ada smiled. "Well, safe travels," she said, turning to rejoin Zane.

"Alright, time to do our part," Diana said.

"We've got this," Yume replied.

The two of them exited the academy, and Diana mounted an ostrock that was waiting for her. Yume floated ahead, with her sparkling smoke dancing behind her, leading the way. The sound of the booming arena faded behind them as they headed for the Deseret of Dreams.

TWENTY-TWO

Yume flew ahead in a cloud of sparkling smoke. Diana held on tight as her ostrock charged forward, keeping the pace. The rhythmic sound of the ostrock's stomping talons in the sand filled her ears. Sabnare's starry night sky and several moons lit the way as they charged through the Desert of Dreams.

"We're on the outskirts of the Baku territory," Yume said.

Diana slowed the pace of her ostrock. They continued following the perimeter of the Desert of Dreams. Hugging the edge of the glowing amethyst mountains until they came to a patch of lavender palms.

"Beyond those trees is where the baku reside. Follow me." Yume floated ahead, leading the way as they entered the trees. They worked their way through the dense coverage of trees until a tiny cove was revealed.

The cove was mostly open, scattered with lavender palms. A tiny waterfall created a stream that emptied into a small pool of water. Caves lined the sides of the purple mountains at varying heights. From deep within the caves, sounds poured out into the clearing. Growing louder as the source grew closer.

Diana's ostrock began to twitch its head, raising its crest as they entered the center of the clearing. Its tail feathers began to rise as it activated its protective barrier. Diana reached down, petting the agitated creature, calming it down. Its feathers unruffled as Diana dismounted and led it forward.

Baku entered the cove en masse. Appearing in puffs of smoke and spilling out of caves. Some stampeded on the ground, while others took to the air. All of them directly headed for Diana and Yume. The baku herd filled in around them as Yume calmly landed in front of Diana, while the ostrock twitched nervously. The herd began to part, making way for Daichi and Eiji.

"What news do you bring us, Yume?" bellowed Daichi.

Yume stepped forward. "It's much worse than we had imagined. Benjiro is dead."

The herd began to trumpet and roar in a mix of anger and sadness. Some collapsed to the ground in tears. Daichi's body shook, and deep blue smoke blasted from his body with rage. Eiji held back the tears welling up in his eyes. His normally vibrant yellow smoke muddied with grey.

The hairs on Diana's arms stood up as the bellowing resonated throughout her body. Shaking her to her core.

"The soothsayer took his life to absorb his powers so that she can take the powers of sandmen. We need to put a stop to this; we need your help to take back the castle and save Sabnare."

"Why should we believe you?" Daichi retorted. "Why should we trust you when you bring this *witch* into our home?" The destain spewed from his mouth.

"She speaks the truth!" Rang out a voice from the crowd.

The group of baku that Yume released from the dungeon, led by Takeshi, stepped into the clearing.

"Without her help, we would have also fallen victim to the soothsayer's plot. Her strength and determination are remarkable," said Takeshi.

Daichi laughed. "Yume, remarkable? I'd hardly think so."

"Brother, hear him out," Eiji said. Giving Daichi a serious look.

Takeshi continued. "Yume refused to leave us behind; she summoned all of her might, releasing great power to set us free."

Daichi paused. Looking from the rescued baku and back over to Yume. She stood before him, trunk held high. Her smoke sparkled, billowing with confidence. He looked at his brother.

"What do you think brother?"

"I think we should hear them out, there has been such great loss," Eiji replied. "It is time for us all to come together to protect our home."

"And you witch, what do you think?"

"I think if we don't all come together, there will be nothing left to protect. Sabnare is a part of all of us, and we need to do whatever we can to protect it."

Daichi stared into Diana's eyes. Her passion emanated from the core of her being. He glanced over the herd of baku, sitting at attention. Takeshi's intense stare was unwavering. Eiji's eyes were kind and reassuring. Looking down at the ground, Daichi released a sigh from his trunk.

"There does not seem to be any choice here. Together, we shall protect Sabnare."

The bellowing of baku filled the air in celebration. Yume reached out her trunk to a reluctant Daichi.

"Thank you for joining us," she said. "Together, we can take back our home."

"I hope you're right." He replied, releasing her trunk.

"I think it's time I head back to the village," Diana said, walking over to Yume.

"Excellent, I'll handle everything here, stay safe."

Diana hugged Yume before mounting her ostrock. As she neared the edge of the cove, Diana looked over her shoulder to see Yume with the full attention of the Baku herd. The corner of her mouth rose into a smile as she rode off back to the village.

TWENTY-THREE

"Make sure those straps are tight," Zane called down to Raza as he was securing ostrock to a sorina.

"Got it covered," Raza replied, moving on to the next ostrock.

Zane turned to Ada. "How are the preparations on the inside of the sorina?"

"All non-essential equipment and fixtures have been removed to make the sorinas lighter. We will be able to move across the Desert of Dreams much faster," she replied, "and now the last pieces of essential equipment are being loaded currently."

"Excellent," he turned to Diana, "and things are set with the baku?"

"All set. Yume and the others are just awaiting our signal."

"Wonderful, Ada, alert the troops that we leave in twenty."

"Yes, Zane," and with a nod and a swirl of smoke, she was off.

Zane walked over to the front of the sorina and looked down to watch everyone hustle to finish preparations. Diana stood beside him. He smiled at her. A sense of peace washed over his face momentarily. "Are you ready?"

Diana brushed a strand of hair out of her face and looked at him. "If somebody had told me a week ago that I'd be fighting a war in a magical land while trying to find my father, who's a sandman, I probably wouldn't have believed them," she chuckled. "But you know, as much as I wish I had more time to prepare and process, I feel confident in a way I've never felt before."

"It's because you're able to embrace yourself fully for the first time. A huge part of yourself was hidden away from everyone, including you, for a very long time. That's going to have a negative subconscious effect and hinder many aspects of your life."

"At first, I didn't think I could do it."

"Truthfully, I had my reservations. I thought I could do it myself, but I believed in Warrick. You were the spark we needed to bring everyone together. It's clear that there are great things in store for you, Diana, and it's an honor to be a part of it."

Diana smiled and wiped a tear from her eye. She watched as people scurried down below, making final preparations.

Raza appeared on the deck, making his way towards Diana and Zane.

"Everything is just about ready," Raza said.

"Excellent, let's double-check the route before we head out," Zane suggested.

"Absolutely," said Diana.

Diana's scroll jumped to life. Its wings flapping, hovering in front of them. An image of Sabnare appeared on the parchment.

"We will ride this way towards the oasis," Zane said, tracing a path on the map that appeared on the scroll as he did. "Once we pass the oasis and reach about here, Diana, you'll need to summon the baku." The scroll marked that spot on the path. "From here, going forward, we will need to be on alert as our presence may be detected by the castle."

Diana nodded, "sounds like a plan."

"I'll make sure that the sorina captains are prepared for anything beyond that point," Raza said.

Raza took his leave to make the final preparations. Diana stared at the map as the scroll floated before her. It all seemed so simple on paper. She had all of the power of Sabnare behind her. Hopefully, that would be enough.

TWENTY-FOUR

The light of the moons of Sabnare shone down as the sorina armada charged through the mountain pass that led to the Desert of Dreams. Sandmen were posted along all sides of the decks, helping to shift the sand and navigating through the glowing, craggy cavern while the tethered ostrock pulled. Raza led the charge on his brilliant white ostrock. Several additional mounted sandmen wove between the ships as they moved across the sand. Diana, Zane, and Ada stood at the front of the lead sorina. Diana's scroll floated nearby, tracking the journey.

The armada burst from the canyon into the expanse of the Desert of Dreams. Following the edge of the mountain range that encircled the desert, the fleet picked up speed. Diana saw the hidden baku cove pass in a blur.

"The sorinas are moving so much faster than our last trip," Diana said.

"Sorinas aren't built for speed," Zane replied, "but removing all the nonessential pieces and adding the extra sandmen and ostrock sure is making quite the difference."

Diana saw Ada looking out over the sea of sand. Her locks flowed behind her in the breeze. In the distance, something was forming on the horizon. It was the oasis, much like an island in the middle of an ocean. The oasis became clearer as they quickly approached. The lavender palms reached up towards the stars from the sand.

Raza gave a signal and began to lead the fleet around the oasis. The sandmen on deck shifted waves of sand, guiding the great ships. The ostrock squawked, following the direction of the mounted sandmen, pulling into the turn. Diana watched as they tore past the palms and the jagged purple crystals left from the battle with the slumbra. The rest of the sorinas followed suit, keeping pace with the lead ship. The armada came out of the turn, now on a direct course to the castle.

"It's almost time," Zane said, glancing at the scroll before looking back at the expansive desert before him.

They rode on through the waves of sand. The sounds of squawking from the ostrock and their heavy footsteps blended with the sounds of shifting sand. In the distance, the Diamond of Dreams appeared over the horizon.

Diana looked over at Ada. "Are you ready?"

Ada nodded and looked forward.

Diana held Ada's bottle high in a battle stance. "I wish the baku would join us!"

Ada raised her arms above her head as her eyes and jeweled cuffs began to glow. Her hair began to dance as the magic energy moved around her. Purple smoke gathered above her, forming a cloud of magic. She thrust her arms out and down to her sides, dissipating the smoke. The energy around her settled as the glowing of her eyes and cuffs subsided.

Puffs of smoke began to form around the armada as the baku joined. Some ran along with the ostrock. Others took to the sky, with a trail of smoke forming as they flew along. More baku appeared on the decks of the sorinas. Diana was able to spot Daichi, Eiji, and Takeshi among the baku appearing among the sorinas. There was still one face she hadn't spotted.

A swirl of smoke appeared behind Diana as Yume appeared. Diana knelt to hug her. Yume wrapped her trunk around her, completing the embrace.

"The castle is in view," Zane said.

The castle's towers stretched up, peaking over the horizon. Its magnificence complementing that of the Diamond of Dreams itself. Diana stood up and gazed upon the castle looming in the distance. She closed her eyes and took a few deep breaths to center herself. The calm slowly passed down her body like warm honey. She opened her eyes, ready to face whatever awaited them.

In the distance, a disturbance manifested in the sand. Dark shadowy limbs reached up from the ground. An army of dreamon had begun rising from the desert, blocking the path to the castle.

"Dreamon!" shouted Zane shouting the alarm.

The baku began to trumpet as they charged. The ostrock raised their tail feathers, now glowing with magical energy, creating a barrier to protect the armada. The ostrock-mounted sandmen began to shift walls of sand into the dreamon while baku began to devour them.

The dreamon were unrelenting. Swiping at baku and sandmen with their long, spindly arms and fingers. Baku exploded into smoke as dreamon impaled them, extending their fingers together like a lance. Others grabbed sandmen, absorbing them between the vinelike coils of their bodies, never to be seen again.

Eiji took to the sky. His yellow smoke streaked behind as he dive-bombed a slashing dreamon, his trunk ready to feed. He crashed into the dreamon, pinning it to the ground. The dreamon trashed about as Eiji fed. The dreamon's featureless face disappeared as it was sucked up by Eiji's trunk.

Another dreamon attacked a couple of mounted sandmen, knocking the sandmen from their ostrock. Daichi placed himself between the fallen sandmen and the attacking dreamon. He let out a mighty bellow. He charged, slashing with his one good tusk. The dreamon's blood-curdling cry rang out as Daichi impaled the dreamon. The screeching dreamon dissolved away into black shadowy smoke as it was devoured by Daichi.

A movement in Diana's peripheral caught her attention. A shadow had appeared over the side of the sorina, spreading across the deck. Several dreamon started to surface from the shadow. Their glowing eyes pulsating.

Yume sprang forward, blocking Diana, Zane, and Ada from the forming dreamon.

"Stay back!" Yume shouted.

Yume crouched, ready to charge. The dreamon began to spread out along the deck of the sorina. Slashing their long, sharp fingers at the sandmen who were busy shifting the sand that was guiding the ship. Yume raced forward and circled the dreamon, herding them as she released a sparkling smoke screen. The dreamon howled in confusion as they gathered together.

Yume jumped out of the smoke, catching the dreamon by surprise. Her smoke flared as she sucked up the dreamon like a vacuum. They clawed at the deck of the sorina in desperation. Trying to fight the powerful suction until there was nothing left of the shadowy figures except for splintered claw marks.

"Great job, Yume," Zane said.

"I'm going to make a sweep of the deck to check for more dreamon," Yume said as she flew off in a swirl of pink smoke.

Mounted sandmen on the ground continued the shifting of sand. They created great walls of moving sand, knocking into dreamon and clearing a path.

A wall of sand crashed into one of the sorinas, sending Diana falling over the side.

"Diana!" Ada shouted as she conjured a cloud of smoke to cushion her fall.

Diana stood up, brushing off the sand. A dreamon rose from the sand beneath her feet, reaching out to grab her. She shifted the sand, knocking it away. It crashed backward, scratching her arm as it fell.

Diana winched in pain, grabbing her arm as she watched the sorinas continue towards the castle, leaving her behind.

She began to sand-surf to catch up with the armada. Weaving between obstacles. Shifting away dreamons. Swerving to avoid a diving baku and panicked ostrock. Diana reached the side of the lead sorina. She focused and began to shift up a wall, raising her higher.

A dreamon reached for her leg as she rose to meet the sorina. A blur of blue and yellow raced by her as Takeshi took out the dreamon. Diana reached the height of the sorina's deck, and with a quick motion, she shifted to the side and leapt towards the deck. Yume reached out to catch her with her trunk and braced Diana's landing.

"Thank you, Yume"

"My pleasure!"

Diana marched to the front of the sorina. Zane and Ada stood there deflecting dreamon. Diana surveyed the area, then turned to the scroll. "What's the situation?" she asked.

The scroll showed the numbers of dreamon dwindling and retreating. In a corner of the scroll's parchment, it showed losses of life. They had managed to keep casualties to a minimum, but the loss was still a tough pill to swallow. Diana clenched her fist, holding back tears. She shook her head, knowing that now was not the time to lose focus.

Zane saw the look on Diana's face. He reached for her hand, squeezed it, and said, "Let's finish this."

TWENTY-FIVE

The armada came to a halt in front of the moat surrounding the castle. The sorinas parked side by side, creating an imposing wall of force. Raza led the mounted ostrock as they began to circle and create a perimeter around the group.

A great screech came from above. Delfina circled above the castle grounds in her owl form. Her wings pulled in, and she dived down towards the group. She landed on the bridge of the moat facing the armada.

Delfina's owl form began to melt away as she rose from the ground. Her feathers fused together, forming robes that danced in the gentle Sabnare breeze. The sharp beak softened into lips, revealing the true nature of her face. The corner of the soothsayer's mouth raised into a defiant grin.

Diana looked at Ada. Ada nodded. With a swirl of smoke, Diana, Zane, Ada, and Yume appeared on the ground in front of the fleet. Sandmen from the other sorina's appeared before their respective ships. Baku flew up above the rest. Diana stepped forward. Her eyes locked on the soothsayer.

"Delfina," she shouted, "This is your last chance to tell me what you've done with Warrick and leave Sabnare peacefully."

Delfina's face was painted with confusion and then twisted into a laugh.

"I haven't done anything to Warrick yet. But I am not leaving until I get what is mine and make him pay for what he has done to me. None of you will stop me," she yelled.

"Have it your way." Diana retrieved the book of spells from her robes, flipping to the dog-eared page that marked a banishing spell. She held out her projective hand, holding the book in her other, and chanted.

"In this place, you can no longer be . . ." The magic spread through her body like a wave warming her body. The sand at Delfina's feet began to stir. "I call the magic inside of me . . ." The sand began to rise like a cyclone, picking up speed. "No longer for us to be face to face . . ." Delfina's body was now completely obstructed by the whirling sand. "I expel you now from this place. Banished be!"

The cyclone of sand swirled faster and faster, rising high into the air. Magic energy crackled like lightning, and the wind made a deafening howl. The castle was no longer visible, obstructed by the storm.

Diana's robes billowed violently around her. Bits of sand pelting her in the face. Diana focused all her might. The energy continued to gather in her palm, growing warmer as it gathered.

The party behind her took a step back as the sandstorm raged.

Diana gave a final push and released the built-up magical energy inside, collapsing to her knees. Her breath labored as she put the book away into her robes and returned to her feet.

Diana watched as the cyclone began to slow. The funnel dwindled and began to sink back into the ground. Her stomach sank.

There stood Delfina. Her hands glowed from deflecting the spell. She cocked her head, a crooked smile plastered on her face, and then laughed. "That's all you have?" she taunted, "you're going to have to do better than that to be rid of me." Delfina let out a victorious cackle.

Diana felt as if she couldn't breathe. Her spell was a failure when everyone was counting on her. Tears welled up in Diana's eyes, threatening to overflow. She shook her head and wiped her eyes. She knew she didn't have time for self-doubt.

"I won't give up. I will defeat you and find my father!" Diana shouted.

"Your father? Warrick is your father?"

Delfina stared Diana down. Her eyes bored into Diana's. A chill ran down Diana's spine.

"So, Warrick sends his daughter instead of facing me himself. How pathetic."

"Pathetic? I'll show you who's pathetic!"

Diana swung her hand, sending a torpedo of sand at the soothsayer. Delfina easily defused the attack before it could reach her.

"Enough of this. I'll destroy you, just as I'll destroy Warrick. And because you're his daughter, I'll hold nothing back. It's time for you to catch some zees!" Delfina yelled while making a motion in the air with her arms.

Diana's blood ran cold. Her body trembled uncontrollably. She stood there, paralyzed with fear, watching the sky appear to go dark.

CHAPTER

TWENTY-SIX

The sound of buzzing filled the air, reverberating through Diana's bones. Her whole body trembled uncontrollably. Sweat ran down her brow; her robes clung uncomfortably against her body. Tears filled Diana's eyes and spilled down her cheeks. Her worst fear loomed before her.

The sky was filled with a cloud of giant purple bees the size of small dogs. The swarm swirled angrily through the air, heading towards the sandmen and baku.

"Don't let the zees sting you!" Zane shouted, preparing to fight.

Diana's eyes darted from side to side. The zees were surrounding the armada. Baku took to the air, striking with their tusks. Sandmen shifted the sand with a fevered intensity. Walls of sand rose from the ground, slamming into zees.

Daichi hoovered in the air, entangled, fighting a zee.

"We can't devour them like dreamon," Daichi grunted.

Daichi charged at the zee. His one good tusk deflected a blow from the zee's massive stinger. The zee buzzed with fury, darting back towards Daichi. The zee prepared to strike, adjusting its angle, and plunged its stinger into the Daichi. He let out a painful trumpet as he began to lose consciousness.

The razor-sharp mandibles of the zee glistened in the moonlight as they clamped around the Daichi's throat. The zee squeezed harder as he struggled. With a final trash, Daichi disintegrated into a blue smoke, dissipating on the breeze.

The brawl intensified. A group of ostrock charged as a flock, shields up, plowing into hordes of zees. Part of the swarm enveloped the ostrock. The frenzied sounds of buzzing and squawks rang out. Zees rammed against the energy shield with such force that the ostrock crumpled to the ground. Feathers scattered into the air. Now that their shields were down, the zees stung the ostrock repeatedly before moving on to their next targets.

Spears of sand shot through the air, missing more zees than they hit, as sandmen shifted from the ground and the decks of the sorinas. Zees continued to swarm, forcing sandmen to dive over the sides of the ships to avoid the vicious attacks.

Baku fought with tusk and trunk, from land and sky. Others created sparkling smoke screens to confuse and conceal.

Diana's head began to ache from the sounds of squawks and bellowing trumpets as they were slaughtered. She stood there frozen in fear and unable to process the carnage around her. Zees were dive-bombing all around, their numbers too high to count. A movement directly in front of her caught Diana's eye. Killer zee was barreling down on her, stinger poised to strike. She let out a shriek, crouched down, and closed her eyes.

Diana went tumbling to the ground. Her side felt like she had just been hit by a car. She spun her head around to see Yume, who had pushed her out of the way. The zee's stinger pierced into Yume, and she fell to the ground.

"Yume!" Diana screamed. Desperately crawling to her fallen friend. She cradled Yume's head. She was not responsive. "Yume, you need to wake up," she cried, shaking her friend. "Wake up, Yume," Diana wailed.

The tears poured out like a busted damn. Sobbing, Diana kept shaking Yume's limp body with increasing desperation. The sounds of the battle around them seemed to vanish. It was just Diana and Yume.

"I'm so sorry, Yume, this is all my fault. If only I was stronger." Diana collapsed on top of Yume. Her chest heaving as she wept.

Slowly, the sounds of the world started to intrude again. That's when she heard it. Laughter. Above the sounds of battle. Laughter. Diana turned to see Delfina. Her laughter assaulted Diana's ears.

Her breathing became heavy. She rose from the ground, clenching her fists. A heat rose in her body as the sand at her feet began to circle her. A purple aura formed around her, kicking up a breeze that tossed around her hair. Her breathing intensified, forcefully exhaling from her nose. Diana let out a scream from the depths of her soul. Her eyes began to glow purple from rage, and orbs of lavender flames manifested in her hands.

The power within Diana surged, and purple fire exploded into the air, taking out several of the zees. Their flaming remains rained down like fireworks while sandmen and baku dodged the barrage of flames.

The purple flames began to dance around Diana's body, with the shifting sands intensifying. The flames turned grains of sand into glass-like shrapnel that tore at her robes and skin. Another surge of power sent flames shooting out from her body in all directions.

The remaining ostrock fanned out their tail feathers. A glowing aura formed, raising a barrier to protect the armada. Walls of sand were shifted by the sandmen to block the onslaught of flames. The intense heat of Diana's flames melted the sand into jagged glass spikes.

Diana screamed as the power surged again, sending a wall of flames into the air, wiping out hundreds of zees. Blasts of fire recklessly shot from hands. The wild flames took out several more of the zees while simultaneously setting two of the sorinas ablaze.

"Take her away!" Delfina shouted while making a signal with her hand.

A group of zees descended on Yume's body. They lifted her off the ground and hauled her towards the castle.

Diana shot flames at the retreating zees, each blast missing its mark. Her powers were surging beyond her control. It felt as if someone else were piloting her body. Her mind was clear of rational thought. All that remained was raw, unchecked emotion.

Diana shot towards Delfina, sand-surfing at a breakneck speed. Hands engulfed in magical purple flames. She pulled back her flaming fist, preparing to strike. She closed in on the soothsayer. Extending her arm as she sped ahead.

In the blink of an eye, Delfina conjured an energy blast to repel Diana. Diana flew into the air and came crashing down, tumbling across the sand.

"You'll have to do better than that," taunted Delfina.

"Watch me," Diana said, her voice booming like thunder.

Diana regained her footing and launched a violent barrage of violet fireballs.

Delfina repelled each blast with a simple wave of her arms. She shifted the sand, grabbing Diana's leg, and slamming her face first into the ground.

Diana started to rise, getting on all fours. The taste of iron filled her senses. She spit out a glob of blood onto the sand. Her lip was busted, and her nose was bleeding. She wiped the blood off her face.

Diana felt the power surging within her. Her glowing eyes intensified. Sparks like lightning shot from corners.

The sand shifted beneath her hand, becoming dense. She stood up as the sand continued to extend from her hand and take shape. Purple flames shot from her hand, engulfing the sand. She raised it high above her head as the violet inferno raged. In a fluid motion, she brought down her arm, expelling the flames to reveal a glowing sword of purple glass.

The sword gave off the same light as the mountains that

surrounded Sabnare. The hilt, forged from the iron in her blood that mixed with the sand, had purple crystals in the cross guard. Tiny magical sigils were etched across the blade.

"Dream shield!" She cried. The dream catcher jumped from her side, spinning as it transformed into a shield. Sand-surfing with all her might, she blasted forward. Diana raised her sword, prepared to strike. As the soothsayer came into range, Diana slashed with all her might.

Delfina manifested a sword to block the blow, repelling Diana's sword. Delfina spun around to strike, only to be blocked by Diana's shield. Diana hacked at Delfina, but she dodged it with ease.

"So much for Warrick's chosen one."

Delfina sprung forward, landing a blow, slicing through Diana's robes and upper arm.

"Argh," Diana screamed in pain as she fell to the ground. The glow of her eyes began to dim as the surging power started to recede. She lay there bloody and panting as the soothsayer loomed over her.

With a wave of her hand, Delfina's sword returned to the unmanifest.

"Give it up, and stop wasting my time. You're not strong enough to defeat me."

Diana watched helplessly as she changed back into an owl. She took to the sky and headed back towards the castle, leaving the raging battle and all its carnage behind her.

CHAPTER

TWENTY-SEVEN

"Are you alright?"

Diana turned to see Ada, followed by Zane. Shaken from the battle, her lip quivered.

"I don't know."

"Here, let us help you up," Zane said as he and Ada attended to Diana.

Ada looked over Diana's wounds, "Here, let me clean you up a bit." With a wave of her hand. Tiny wisps of purple smoke danced across Diana's injuries. The bleeding stopped, and the wounds sealed. She was still a bit swollen and bruised, including her spirit.

"Thanks."

Ada smiled through her concern.

"We need to press on," Zane declared, "Raza and the others have the zees occupied."

Diana looked back at the battlefield. The number of zees had greatly diminished, but so had their allies. The threat wasn't over, but they continued to fight valiantly. The battlefield lay scorched and smoking while sorinas continued to burn in the moonlight.

Zane led the way as they rushed towards the castle. The wood from the bridge creaked beneath their feet as they crossed over the moat. A couple of rouge zees blocked their path in the courtyard.

Zane shifted a wall of sand, knocking one out of the air. The second charged forward. Diana's heart pounded. She raised her sword and sliced through the zee. It exploded into a burst of sand. Diana turned to the zee that Zane grounded. It regained its senses and returned to the air. With a well-aimed fireball, the zee vanished.

Diana retrieved the scroll from her robes. It fluttered to life, hovering in front of them. A layout of the castle appeared on the ancient parchment. A marker showed that Yume was being held in the dungeon, and Delfina was in the center of the castle.

"Looks like the soothsayer is in the sand vault. Diana, you and Ada go after her, and I will go find Yume." Zane looked from Diana to Ada, holding that final glance. "Be careful, who knows what she has protecting her."

Zane ran over to the doorway that would lead to the dungeon. He paused and turned back to take a last glance at Diana and Ada; the concern was painted across his face. With a deep breath, he turned back towards the dungeon to rescue Yume.

Diana and Ada studied the path the scroll had created on the map. The entrance to the sand vault was on the other side of the castle. They needed to take the hallway just to the side of the castle's main doors.

As they approached the hallway, three bewitched guards appeared. Their eyes were cloudy and soulless. Two stood back, blocking the entrance with crystal-tipped spears. The third shot forward, sand-surfing. He shifted an expanding wall of sand in front of him, acting like a bulldozer to clear the way.

Ada quickly made a gesture with her hands. A whirlwind of smoke encompassed Diana and Ada. They disappeared and reappeared as the charging sandman passed. Diana turned and shifted his sand wall back on him, knocking him out.

The other guards charged with their spears. Diana countered, deflecting with her sword and shield. Ada dodged and then blocked the attacks with energy shields from her bangles.

A well-placed strike to her dream shield sent Diana to the ground. She shifted the sand to rise beneath the attacking guard. The guard maintained his balance on the shifting sand and used his leverage to strike. He jumped into the air, holding the spear with both hands tip down. He pulled back. The spear's tip glistened above his head as he used his extra force to strike toward Diana.

The spear disappeared in a waft of smoke. Diana raised her shield, blocking the sandman from toppling over her. She shoved him to the side while scurrying to her feet. She pulled back and struck him in the head with the hilt of her sword. Rendering him unconscious.

"Thanks for the assist," she said to Ada, who had unarmed the guards.

"No problem."

They turned to the final guard. Pillars of sand shot up. Dancing like a fountain. Diana reached out, trying to counter the shift. The erratic movement of the sand made it difficult to focus and subdue the dancing sand.

Ada sent blasts of energy at the jets of sand. For everyone she took out, another appeared. Diana shot blasts of fire. Even that was unable to overtake the sand spouts.

Diana and Ada watched and dodged as the sand's fury increased. Pillars rising and falling all around them. A geyser of sand sprouted up below Diana, making her stumble. She thought about how the other guard had used the sand to attack from above.

"Ada, the sand is too wild for me to shift. Help me get up and above."

Ada looked at the guard and back at Diana. She made a motion with her sword. Ada took a moment to process her plan.

"I've got you."

Ada made a dismissive hand gesture towards Diana. She vanished with a puff of smoke. The bewitched guard looked around with his dull eyes and perplexed face. The sands calmed slightly with his distraction.

Diana jumped out of a cloud of smoke that formed above the guard. There was a large cracking sound as the hilt made contact with the sandman's skull. The pillars of sand collapsed to the ground along with the sandman's unconscious body.

"Well done," remarked Ada.

"I couldn't have done it without you."

They ran past the fallen sandmen and into the hallway. The scroll flew ahead with its leathery wings, leading the way. Streaks of light raced past them from the glowing crystals that lit the hall. Diana and Ada made their way until the hallway emptied into a large open room.

Diana and Ada stopped in their tracks. Dreamon stood in the center of the room. Their blank, featureless faces turned to stare at the women who just entered the room, their glowing eyes intensifying. Spindly limbs reached out, clawing at the air as the shadowy creatures moved towards the doorway.

Diana whipped up a sandstorm. It violently swirled, surrounding the dreamon. Ada summoned smoke that poured from her hands. The smoke mixed with the storm, obscuring the view of the dreamon. Diana took stock of the room. There were several doorways on each side. The scroll showed the path they needed was on the other side of the room. Diana reached out and focused. She drew the sands closer together, tightening the storm, condensing the dreamon in the center of the room.

"Alright, we have a better path now, let's move."

Ada agreed, and they hastily made their way around the raging storm towards the exit. A dreamon's hand reached out of the sand, blocking their path. The dreamon's other hand materialized along with the top of its head. Pulling itself up and out of the sand like a swimmer on the edge of a pool.

"More dreamon are on the way!" shouted Ada.

More hands reached up from the sand in pools of shadow. The

dreamon had begun to slip under the sandstorm in the center of the room.

Diana blasted fireballs at the rising dreamon. The fire sizzled against the twisted, dark flesh, holding back their ascent.

They leapt over it and through the doorway. One of the dreamon followed as it struggled its way to the surface. Ada turned back and summoned a huge smoke screen, filling the room. A portion of the smoke screen poured down one of the adjacent hallways. Ada's bangles pulsed with bright purple light as she conjured a wall that blocked the doorway.

"Let's move; I sent a smoke trail down a different hallway to throw them off."

The scroll flew ahead of them, showing the way. Moving along with all the twists and turns. The sand crunching beneath their feet. The map on the scroll showed they were approaching the end of the hallway.

"Looks like we're almost there," Diana said.

"Keep your guard up."

A muffled sound echoed off the sandy walls of the hallway. As they got closer, the sound became clearer, turning into a low buzzing. A buzzing that grew louder and louder.

They entered a room with a high ceiling. A swarm of several zees hovered above them. Their wings buzzed in agitated fury. That's when Diana saw it. Her blood ran cold, and she began to shake. A zee at least four times the size of the others. It perched high above, where the wall and ceiling met.

"That must be a queen zee," Ada gasped.

Diana's mouth hung open. Two zees dropped down, stingers bared. The bangles around Ada's wrist glowed purple as she shielded herself from the blow and blasted them back. The zees were momentarily stunned before attacking again. The buzzing grew louder with anger.

"Diana, get yourself together!" she yelled over the deafening noise.

Diana shook her head, regathering herself. "Sorry about that."

"They seem to be more aggressive than the ones before. It must be because of the queen."

Diana's legs trembled as she made her way further into the room. A zee dove towards her. She deflected its stinger with her sword. It rebounded and struck again as Diana blocked with her shield. She sliced at the zee, severing its abdomen, and it dissolved into sand.

The zees continued to descend in waves.

Chaos reigned. Flashes of purple and black zipped around. The swarm attacked kamikaze style, diving from above. Diana slashed and blocked. Ada fired blast after blast of energy. The zees dodged the attacks, their rage building.

Diana scanned her surroundings. The room offered no shelter from the barrage. Her mind raced. *There has to be something we can do.* Then it hit her.

"Ada, smoke!" Diana shouted.

Ada's eyes squinted, then opened with a moment of clarity. She raised her hands, filling the area above them with her purple smoke. Diana hoped it would work. The buzzing of the zees tempered down. The smoke had begun to calm the zees.

"Great idea," Ada said.

"I thought since smoke calms bees, the same may work for the zees."

Diana and Ada worked together to clear the room of the zees. Ada's blasts stunned, while Diana's sword quickly eviscerated the more docile zees until the last worker zee burst into sand. It's remains mixing with the smokey air.

Diana and Ada had no time to rest. Thunderous buzzing reverberated throughout the chamber. The queen zee beat her gossamer wings until they were a blur. Dispersing the smoke from the room.

The queen zee glared from its corner. It had a row of imposing spikes leading down its abdomen. At its tip, a stinger pulsed in and out, venom dripping. A set of three spikes adorned its head like a deadly crown. The queen dropped down from above, snapping its serrated mandibles. Its dark purple eyes locked on to Diana.

The queen zee thrust forward its abdomen. Like a bullet, a stinger launched from the queen zee. Barreling towards Diana.

As Diana blocked the stinger with her shield, the force of its impact slid her backward in the sand as it fell to the ground. She watched as a new stinger appeared in its place.

Ada conjured smoke around the queen zee's head. The queen buzzed with rage. It pulled back, shaking its head to clear the smoke. It dove towards Ada. Sand fell from the ceiling as the queen zee landed with a thud. It reached out, violently smacking Ada into a wall with its front leg.

Diana sprinted towards the queen. She drew back her sword and struck the zee on its armored leg. The sword bounced off without leaving a scratch. Diana stumbled back with the sword's rebound. The queen zee returned to the air, shooting a barrage of stingers at Diana. Diana dodged swiftly, sand-surfing around the chamber.

The stingers torpedoed past. Barely missing. Leaving tears in Diana's robes as they grazed the fabric.

Ada stood back up. Her bangles shone bright as she shot into the air. Her bottom half was covered in smoke that trailed behind her as she flew. She dove at the zee, fists glowing with power. She released a blast, knocking the queen zee to the ground. It shot a stinger up at Ada. Ada dodged but crashed into a wall. Sending her tumbling to the ground.

The zee regained its footing and returned to the air, heading for Ada.

Diana looked around the room, trying to figure out a plan of attack. The queen's stingers were scattered around the floor. Inspiration struck Diana. She focused her mind; the magic inside her churned, building. Sand shifted around the stringers, angling them up. Aimed at the queen zee.

Diana threw a fireball at the zee to get its attention. The queen zee zipped around to look at Diana. She blasted another fireball.

Hitting the queen directly in its face. The zee buzzed in anger. Shaking and clawing at its face. It darted towards Diana.

With an upward motion from her arms, Diana released the energy inside her. The sand shifted up. Launching the stingers through the air like javelins, tearing through the queen zee's wings and body.

The queen zee buzzed ferociously as it crashed to the ground. Its tattered body lay in a heap, oozing into the sand. The queen zee tried to stand. Its legs wobbled beneath it before giving way, and the queen zee melted into a pile of sand. The horrific buzzing faded. Leaving the labored breath of Diana and Ada as the only sound in the chamber.

TWENTY-EIGHT

Diana and Ada stood before a great wooden door that led to the sand vault. It towered over them. Ornate in design, hand carved with encrusted crystals. The door prominently featured a scene depicting the Diamond of Dreams. The diamond was surrounded by creatures from Sabnare. Sandmen, genies, baku, dragons, and anthropomorphic cats were among the mix.

Diana pushed on the door, its immense weight refusing to move.

"It's too heavy for me alone, give me a hand."

Ada joined Diana and put all her weight into pushing the door. The door stood firmly in place. Guarding the vault as was intended.

"It's no use, it won't budge," Diana said.

"We will have to shift the door open."

Diana and Ada stepped back. They joined hands, focusing their intent. Their combined energy danced in synchronicity. Sand shifted like waves crashing at the bottom of the door. The waves grew stronger as their power rose.

The current of energy flowed between them. Their emotions blended as one, thoughts and feelings shared freely. They began to act as one. With their free hands, Diana and Ada made a pushing motion. The waves of sand intensified, wearing down the door's determination. The ancient door creaked on its hinges. Slowly opening, just enough to pass through.

The sand vault sat in the center of the castle. It was a huge room that stretched to the top of the tallest tower. Staircases spiraled up to the very top, with several mezzanine levels overlooking the room. The dream sand poured in from the top of the tower like a giant hourglass. Pooling in the center of the room. Several ornate doors lined the perimeter of the dream sand pool.

Delfina stood in the center of the pool. A current of energy leapt from the dream sand to her hands. Her body glowed as the energy swirled around her.

"She's absorbing the energy of the dream sand!" Ada cried.

"Not for long."

Diana made a back-handed swatting motion across her body. A wall of sand sped across the room, slamming into Delfina.

Delfina went flying, her connection severed. She crashed into a door overlooking the pool, crumpling to the ground like a rag doll. Still glowing with an aura of magic.

Diana and Ada ran over. Diana drew back her sword, ready to strike. They stared down at the soothsayer.

"I think she's unconscious," Ada said.

"Let's hope so."

Diana reached down to check on the soothsayer. Delfina's hands retracted into fists. In the blink of an eye, the sand beneath Diana and Ada rose from the pool surrounding them. Binding their limbs to their sides and pulling them back into the ground. Only their heads were exposed above the sand.

Diana struggled beneath the sand, her arms pinned to her side, including her sword that was in hand. She turned to see Ada also fighting against the sand.

"I told you. You're no match for me." Delfina stood up, looking at her glowing arms, turning her hands to see both sides. A crooked smile appeared on her face. She chuckled, "And now it looks like you're too late. So much for the daughter of Warrick." Her laugh besieged Diana's ears.

Delfina ran over to the stairs on the other side of the room and began to climb. Working her way up. Spiraling around the tower. Delfina reached the final landing, exiting through a doorway near the top of the tower.

Diana continued to struggle. She focused deep within herself. She could feel heat spread across her body as the magic began to focus. She tried to shift the sand. Nothing. She tried again to move her arms and direct the sand. Her body was completely immobilized from the neck down.

"I can't shift the sand; can you get free?" Dian asked.

"I can't. The dream sand is confining our powers, acting like an insulator. I can't even revert to smoke."

Ada struggled some more. Then, suddenly turned to face Diana.

"Do you still have my bottle on you?"

"Yeah, it's in my satchel."

"Then you need to wish us out. It should be able to offset the dream sand's magic."

Diana focused. She struggled beneath the sand. The fingers of her free hand gathered her robes, making her way to the satchel beneath it. Diana felt a smooth surface as her finger traced the opening of the bottle.

"I wish we were free from the dream sand!"

Ada's eyes began to glow. Their bodies transformed into smoke and swirled up and out of the dream sand. The streams of smoke swirled together like a dance and landed in front of the staircase. The smoke dissipated, revealing Diana and Ada.

"We need to stop her," Diana said, running up the stairs.

The pair followed the soothsayer up the stairs. Spiraling higher and higher. Sand cascaded down from the Diamond of Dreams, rushing past them and filling the pool below.

Diana's foot slipped as a piece of the stairs crumbled beneath it. Her body tumbled over the edge, dropping her sword as she fell.

Ada's hand reached out and grabbed Diana's as her body crashed into the wall. Ada helped her back onto the stairs.

"Are you alright?" Ada asked.

"Yeah, I'm fine. Let's keep moving."

Diana and Ada reached the doorway at the top. They stepped out onto a large platform at the top of the tower, flanked by the battlement wall. The Diamond of Dreams hovered above them. Its power and beauty were unfathomable. It slowly rotated, sparkling in the still night sky. Reflections of Sabnare's several moons could be seen in its facets. Dream sand poured out of its glowing aura from the point at the bottom. Dropping through the hole in the center of the platform.

Delfina stood on the opposite end of the platform. Her arms were outstretched, taking in the diamond's aura.

Diana summoned a fireball into her hand and hurtled it at Delfina. The aura from the Diamond of Dreams swirling around her deflected the attack.

"She's connected to the diamond, and it's protecting her!" Ada growled.

Diana tried again to no avail.

"Stop interfering," said a voice from the stairwell. "I have everything under control."

Diana and Ada turned to see Malvin as he stepped into the doorway. His face was twisted in anger. His dull purple eyes stared daggers at Diana.

"You call this under control?" Ada said, gesturing towards Delfina.

"Don't speak to me like that, you wretched genie."

"You really think you can stop us?" Diana said, summoning a fireball in her hand.

"I have my ways," he sneered, yanking the chains he held in his hands.

Zane and Yume stumbled forward, bound by Malvin's chains.

"Zane..." Ada said under her breath while slightly reaching out her hand.

Diana extinguished her fire.

"I thought you might see it my way."

Malvin yanked the chains, throwing Zane and Yume into the wall. He raised his arms and made a pointing gesture towards the wall with both hands. "Ad catenam!"

Links of sand jumped from the wall, turning into glowing purple chains. The chains wrapped around Diana and Ada, strapping them to the wall. Zane and Yume's chains leapt up, joining them next to the others.

The wind picked up, whipping up sand and debris. The Diamond of Dreams spun faster above them as the energy swirling around Delfina intensified.

Diana struggled against the chains. Ada kept trying to smoke out but couldn't free herself from her bondage. Yume shook and bellowed from her trunk. Zane's neck muscles clenched while straining against the confinement.

"Struggle all you like," Malvin spat. "Any moment now, Delfina will be fully connected to the Diamond of Dreams, and this will all be over."

An energetic vortex raged around them like a cyclone. Purple lightning sparked around the Diamond of Dreams. The violent winds caused dream sand to whip around as it tried to fall to the pool below.

"How can you let her do this to our home, our people?" Zane cried out.

Malvin glared at Zane.

"I'm doing this to protect them!" He shouted. "Cleaning up the mess that Warrick created with his negligence. It's his fault that she lost her ability to see visions of the future. Once the Diamond of Dreams restores her, she will leave."

Diana's eyes widened. Her stomach dropped. *Warrick stripped her of her ability?* Even so, Diana couldn't believe that Malvin would think this was any way to set things right.

Delfina let out a cackle, "I can feel it, my power returning!"

The Diamond of Dreams spun wildly, rocking side to side in a chaotic dance, its facets a blur. The river of energy poured into Delfina's third eye chakra. The severed connections of her powers were healing and expanding beyond anything they had been before.

"We need to hurry before she completely drains the Diamond of Dreams!" Ada cried.

Diana struggled against the chains. Her hand was pinned against Ada's bottle.

"I wish we had a way to sever the connection," Diana said without realizing her word choice.

Ada's eyes began to glow with a purple blaze. Her illuminated bangles absorbed the chains that bound them to the wall. She took to the sky, her lower body shrouded by smoke. An aura of magic surrounded her with blinding intensity. She thrust her head back as her platinum locks came alive with the energy. Arms aimed at the Diamond of Dreams; her bangles let out a devastating blast.

The Diamond of Dreams wobbled on its axis. Light pulsed from the center of the diamond, glowing brighter with every flash. Its dazzling light illuminated the sky. It was as close to daylight as Sabnare had ever seen. The whirring sound of the storm around the spinning gem was deafening.

A final energy pulse rocked the Diamond of Dreams, causing it to explode. Ada fell from the sky, her energy waning as the blast rendered everyone unconscious. A shrapnel of shards rained down over the castle and across the Desert of Dreams. The tower shook violently as the castle shifted on its foundation. Everyone plummeted through the open hole in the floor, their bodies tumbling as they raced to meet the ground.

TWENTY-NINE

Diana blinked her eyes as she started to come to. Struggling to sit up, she rubbed her head, trying to ease the throbbing. She looked around, trying to gather her senses. As her vision cleared, Diana's surroundings came into focus. She was sitting in the dream sand pool.

Wide, jagged cracks ran up the walls, splaying out in different directions. Chunks of the staircases were missing, along with significant portions of the mezzanine levels. Several of the ornate doors that surrounded the pool hung crooked in their frames, with a few missing completely. To her side, Malvin lay unconscious. A bruise was starting to form on his forehead where a shard of the Diamond of Dreams had hit him.

Diana rose to her feet, scanning the pool, and spotted Ada a few feet away. Diana rushed over and knelt by her side.

"Wake up, Ada," she said, gently shaking her sister.

Ada's eyes slowly opened. Squinting, trying to see, she looked at Diana.

"What happened?"

"The Diamond of Dreams exploded."

Ada's mouth dropped open in horror.

A moaning sound came from the other side of the pool. Diana and Ada followed the direction of the sound. Zane lay there, beginning to stir, next to Yume. Diana woke Zane with a gentle shake. He rubbed his eyes, blinking at Diana.

"How long was I out?"

"I'm not sure."

Zane looked around. The vault was forged to be the strongest part of the castle. He tried to process the massive damage afflicting the chamber, which now looked on the brink of collapse.

Diana turned her focus to Yume. Ada sat at her side, stroking her back to wake her. Muffled sounds came from her trunk, and small amounts of sparkling smoke appeared around her ankles. Yume labored to her feet and shook like a dog trying to dry off. Her large, bright eyes filled with sadness and worry as she saw the cracks that ravaged the sides of the tower.

"If you're ok, I need to check on the rest of the castle and make sure everyone is alright," Zane said.

"I want to come too," Yume chirped.

"I'm alright if you are Ada," Diana replied.

"We'll be fine," Ada said, looking down at the ground. "Please be careful."

Zane reached out and cupped her hand.

"We will be safe."

Zane kissed Ada on the cheek before releasing her hand and going off with Yume to check the castle.

Diana noticed Delfina lying a few yards behind Ada.

"Look, there's the soothsayer!"

Delfina's body splayed out on the ground. Discarded and tossed aside. The once imposing soothsayer now appeared fragile and worn. Diana leaned in for a closer look. Delfina's chest rose and fell.

"She's breathing."

Delfina's eyes started to open. As her vision returned, she saw

Diana. She sat up quickly and made a motion with her hands, trying to dispel her. Diana stood there, unaffected. Delfina's powers were too weak after being disconnected from the Diamond of Dreams.

"It's over, we stopped you."

Delfina glared at Diana. Her loathing burned deep. She tried her powers again to no avail.

"What did you do? My magic isn't working!" she cried. Delfina looked at her hand in front of her, trembling. Tears welled up in her eyes. "You've taken everything from me!" she sobbed, "I'll never let you win. You're even worse than Warrick. I will get back everything you people have stolen from me."

"We aren't going to let you hurt anyone else," Diana said.

The scroll jumped from her side. Its wings fluttered as it opened. The scroll revealed a spell across its parchment. Diana read the information presented by the scroll. She reached down, scooping a heaping amount of dream sand into her hand as the scroll returned to her robes.

"Litost!"

Diana projected the glowing dream sand at Delfina's face. It spiraled around the soothsayer's head, invading every available orifice.

Delfina screamed in pain, holding her head, trying to block the sand from penetrating. Disturbing images flashed through her mind. She fell back to the ground, writhing in the sand, weeping from the depths of her soul.

Every drop of her own misery flooded to the surface. A hurricane of torment assaulted her psyche. Tears gave way to unhinged laughter and back to screams as the spell tore through her mental fabric. Delfina stopped rolling in agony as her cognitive abilities faded to blank. A vacant smile spread across her face. She settled on the ground, tears rolling down her face, dripping into the sand.

"I think you may have overpowered it," Ada said, "you may have broken her mind."

They stared down at the empty husk of the soothsayer. The sand swirled around her, and she disappeared in a flash of light.

"Where did she go?" Diana asked.

"I sent her away."

Diana and Ada turned to see Malvin stand behind them.

Malvin looked around at the damage that surrounded them. He turned towards the place where the Diamond of Dreams used to be. His face turned red as he clenched his fists.

A glint in the sand behind Malvin caught Diana's eye. Her sword stood there, sticking out of the sand, only a few yards away.

"Do you have any idea of the damage you have done?" he shouted. "If you had only stayed away and minded your own business, everything would have worked out. Now you've obliterated the Diamond of Dreams, jeopardizing the balance of every realm."

"It wasn't on purpose all I wanted to do was save Sabnare."

"And now you've destroyed it. You're reckless, just like Warrick. Acting without thinking."

Diana kept her eyes focused on Malvin while carefully shifting the sand. Bringing her sword closer. Trying not to catch Malvin's attention.

"Malvin, give her some grace, this is all new to her," Ada said, "We can fix things."

"Don't speak to me, genie! You've all done enough. I will find a way to fix what happened," he paused, "and you are both no longer welcome in Sabnare."

The sword shot out of the sand directly to Diana's hand. She pulled back into a fighting stance. Prepared to strike, her sword glowed brightly.

Malvin raised his hands above his head.

"Expelle terram somniorum!"

A hurricane of sand arose, engulfing Diana and Ada. The sand abrased their skin as it swirled around. Diana could barely see through the kicked-up sand.

"Ada!" she cried, reaching out and for Ada. Ada grabbed her hand and pulled her into a protective embrace.

The wind grew violent as the sandstorm grew tighter. Compacting on itself until it dissipated. The sand settled in the pool, revealing that Diana and Ada were no longer there.

THIRTY

Diana opened her eyes as the whirling storm faded. She stood in a familiar room. A cozy candle-lit room with velvet drapes and posh green furniture. The scent of cinnamon tickled her nose, and the sound of a crackling fire met her ears. Diana and Ada were in the hidden room in her basement.

"Diana!"

Selene rushed over and wrapped her arms around her daughter. Diana dropped her sword and squeezed back as tightly as she could. A sense of relief and sorrow flowed through her. Tears ran down her face, and she began to cry.

"Diana, what's wrong?"

"I made a mess of things," she cried.

"I'm sure it's not that bad."

Selene hugged her daughter, pulling her in tight. She noticed Ada standing behind Diana.

"And who is this?"

"This is Ada," she paused. "She's my sister."

Selene tilted her head with intrigue. Processing the information her daughter just delivered. A sly smile appeared on her face.

"Pleased to make your acquaintance," Ada said, reaching out her hand for Selene's.

"Pleasure to meet you. I'm Selene, Diana's mom," she said, ignoring Ada's hand and going in for a hug.

Ada awkwardly returned the hug. She glanced at Diana, who wiped away her tears and smiled.

Selene led the girls to the seating area. Diana and Ada settled in on the couch while Selene sat across from them in a chair.

"So, tell me what happened."

Diana's lip quivered.

"I wasn't able to find my father. We did manage to stop the soothsayer . . . although, we probably did more damage than we did good."

Diana lowered her head. Selene grabbed her hands.

"What do you mean?"

"Well, in the process of battling the soothsayer, the magic didn't go as planned. We managed to destroy the Diamond of Dreams. Which now puts the balance of all the realms in jeopardy."

Selene paused for a moment, reflecting on what Diana had told her. Choosing her words thoughtfully.

"Not all is lost," Selene said, "If there is one thing I know from my work as a maid, it's that intention is a big part of magic. Rarely is there an instance where good-intentioned magic that goes wrong can't be fixed. That's not to say cleanup is easy. It definitely requires work, but hope is never lost."

She reached out to Diana's chin. Tilting her head up to look her in the eyes.

"I know your heart. I know you did everything you could. Just because things didn't go as planned, that doesn't mean that's what will define you. The steps you take next are what will decide the kind of person that you are."

"I'm not even sure where to start."

"We were also banished from Sabnare," Ada said, "Returning could prove to be quite difficult."

Selene thought about what they said, trying to think of a course of action. Then inspiration struck.

"I know! How about if I get you both set up with a suite at The Germaine?" Selene suggested. "There are so many magical resources there that could be of assistance. I can also book a meeting with Alden, the head of The Germaine. His wealth of knowledge, I'm sure, would prove to be invaluable."

Diana looked at her mom and then at Ada. Ada nodded with her approval. An opportunity had presented itself. An opportunity to fix things. To finish things. *Well, at least I'll have some time to prepare before jumping in.*

"Let's do it, it sounds like a wonderful way to reconvene," Diana said. "Then we will be able to return to Sabnare, correct the damage done, and," she paused, "find our father."

Ada smiled and squeezed her hand.

"Wonderful," Selene said, "I'll go make the arrangements right now, not a moment to waste."

Diana felt a bit of weight lift from her shoulders. She had her mom and her sister. They also had a plan. This time, she would be prepared. The overwhelming feeling she had when she left no longer plagued her. No matter the task, no matter the odds. Soon, she would return to Sabnare.

WANT MORE?

If you enjoyed Desert of Dreams, please consider signing up for my reader list so you can be the first to know about upcoming releases and other updates. When you sign up, you can read my original short story, Tears of the Baku, starring Yume.

Brent Perrotti's Reader List

Acknowledgments

I want to thank everyone who has supported me on this path to publication and has taken the time to read Desert of Dreams. It would mean the world to me if you could leave a review. Nothing helps an indie author's visibility more than reviews. Even if you can't, I'm beyond grateful you decided to follow Diana on her journey into Sabnare.

To all my family and friends who supported and believed in me. Thank you for listening to my ideas and being genuinely excited to read my book.

I also want to give a special shout-out to Kim Chance. Your advice and friendship have made all the difference, and your critique helped me make my story the best it could be.

ABOUT THE AUTHOR

Born and raised in the Chicagoland area, Brent has always had a love of books and stories. For as long as he can remember, he has created interesting characters and amazing worlds for them to inhabit.

When not writing, Brent is an avid knitter and crocheter. He can also be found playing Pokémon and watching anime, RuPaul's Drag Race, or The Golden Girls for the 1,000th time.

Brent currently lives in Chicago with his chihuahuas, cat, and hermit crabs.

http://brentperrotti.com

facebook.com/BrentPerrotti

instagram.com/brent_perrotti

x.com/Brent_Perrotti

tiktok.com/@brent_perrotti

youtube.com/@BrentPerrotti

amazon.com/stores/author/B01MZDYGJO